BOTH SIDES OF THE LAW

A full hand in draw poker changed Hardin's life — and almost ended it. First there was the shoot-out with the house gambler. Then suspicion of bank robbery, enforced recruitment into a posse, gunfights in the hills and pursuit by both sides of the law in strange country. He'd never had so much trouble! What should he do? Drift on, away from this hellhole, or stay and fight? There was no real choice — it was fight or die . . .

HANK J. KIRBY

BOTH SIDES OF THE LAW

Complete and Unabridged

LINFORD
Leicester

First published in Great Britain in 2007 by
Robert Hale Limited
London

First Linford Edition
published 2008
by arrangement with
Robert Hale Limited
London

British Library CIP Data

Kirby, Hank J.
 Both sides of the law.—Large print ed.—
 Linford western library
 1. Western stories
 2. Large type books
 I. Title
 823.9'14 [F]

ISBN 978–1–84782–321–2

Published by
F. A. Thorpe (Publishing)
Anstey, Leicestershire

Set by Words & Graphics Ltd.
Anstey, Leicestershire
Printed and bound in Great Britain by
T. J. International Ltd., Padstow, Cornwall

This book is printed on acid-free paper

1

Last Hand

Hardin was leaning against the clapboard wall of the barber shop, rolling a cigarette and admiring the palomino gelding at the hitch rail, when a deep voice said beside him, 'Throat-cuttin' time, eh?'

A little startled, Hardin flicked his gaze to the man who had appeared alongside him even as he ran his tongue across the edge of the cigarette paper. He finished rolling, smoothed the cylinder and put it in his mouth.

While he searched for a match, he said, 'I don't get it.'

The man held a match for him while he lit up, then fired the half-smoked cigar jammed between his own lips. 'That palomino — makes your mouth water, don't it? Feel like you could cut someone's throat just so's you could have it.'

Hardin smiled crookedly, understanding now. 'Nope. Never wanted anything badly enough to want to cut anyone's throat.'

'That so? Well, takes all kinds.' A puff of aromatic smoke and then a casual question. 'I know you, don't I?'

Hardin turned so he could better see the man now. He was half a head shorter than Hardin, round about the same age — late thirties — but he wore a heavy frontier moustache mottled with nicotine stains. His nose was large and bent in the middle, swinging towards the right. Either side of it were brown eyes that looked candid and friendly enough right now but Hardin had the feeling they could turn to chips of flint that would help thin out those lips at the same time. The hat was greasy and trail-stained and lank dark hair sprouted here and there, almost covering one ear on the left side. The clothes were the regular range outfit, a mite faded and worn, dusty but not much stained. The man was rangy but hard-muscled. Nothing special to look at.

He carried only one gun, but the bullet-belt slanted sharply so that it hung low on the thigh, base of the holster swinging free. Hardin returned his gaze to the man's face — and suddenly a memory stirred.

The man smiled. 'Yeah, Ward Jericho. You recall, eh?'

Hardin nodded slowly, sifting the memory, looking for the hard core of their meeting. 'Station West on the Tombstone Run — hell, three, nearly four years ago!' He shook his head slowly. 'No wonder I feel old some days. You were ridin' shotgun on the Southbound.'

'And you were the guard on the Westbound — Cole Hardin. Bit of a hero. Shot your way past a bunch of Apache renegades, and not one passenger got a scratch — yeah. Bought you a drink in Santiago's bar.'

They shook hands briefly, grinning.

'There was more'n one drink. I kinda recollect the army patrol throwing us in the cells overnight . . . '

Jericho laughed. 'Hell, yeah, an' wakin' us before daylight so's we could get aboard our stages. Man, I hate to think how well I might've guarded them passengers on the Southbound that day, if we'd run into renegades!'

'Me too.' Hardin drew on his cigarette and added quietly, 'Didn't I hear you . . . quit not long after that?'

Jericho shrugged and smiled briefly. 'Quit. Fired — somethin' like that.'

Hardin had heard more too: there had been talk that a hold-up at the river crossing was set-up by Jericho and the three masked bandits who lifted the pay chest no one but the driver and guard were supposed to know about. The driver got himself shot and died later, but, to play it safe, the stageline fired Ward Jericho.

But Hardin didn't mention that he

remembered that part.

'How about you? You're not still ridin' shotgun on the stagelines are you?' Jericho sounded genuinely interested and Hardin shook his head.

'Just drifting now. Work here and there to make a few bucks. Take a break and spend it. When it's gone, find another job.'

Jericho flicked his cigar butt into the hot street, hitching at his gunbelt and thumbing back his hat. 'Tried that for a while. Itchy feet don't get a man anywheres.'

'Aw, I dunno — seen a lot of country. Some I wouldn't mind going back to, some day, and settling down.'

'You need money to settle down.'

'I'll make enough one day — or win enough.'

Jericho arched his shaggy eyebrows. 'You still like a gamble then?'

'I've sat in on a few games, won enough once to spend almost half a year on the drift before I had to go back to real work. Was in California, summertime — I was riding a real lucky streak there for a spell.'

'Never lasts, do it?'

'Never does.'

'You just ridin' through here?'

Hardin nodded slightly. 'In a day or so. Might sit in on a card game tonight. Hear there's one working up in the back room of the Palace. Stakes build up quick, they tell me.'

'Yeah . . . ? Could look in myself. You want a beer?'

Hardin smiled thinly. 'No, thanks. I ain't that flush that I can risk falling into the kinda session with you like I did at Station West. I need all I got for the game.'

Jericho shrugged, taking it good-naturedly, though there were plenty who would be insulted. He thrust his wide shoulders off the wall. 'OK, I gotta meet a couple fellers, anyway. Just could turn into a long session at the bar. Might see you when you're rakin' in the chips tonight.'

'I *hope* that's how you see me. *Adios*, for now.'

Jericho nodded and moved away down the boardwalk. There weren't many folk about in the heat, but this was a prosperous looking town. Rich grazing country all round, some of the hazy blue ranges still showing small caps of snow in the high country, a big river to the north, the Rio Puerco.

Might be a decent-sized stake or two on the poker tables tonight after all, he thought. *He hoped so.*

He could sure use some *dinero*. He hoped the cards would fall right for him and felt his fingers itching for the smooth feel of pasteboards already. He thrust off the wall and moved towards the edge of the boardwalk, catching a glimpse of an old Indian with long white hair hanging below a greasy, battered cavalry hat of ancient vintage. Hardin felt in his pocket, pulled out a half-dollar and two bits. He hesitated, then held out the half-dollar in front of the Indian's seamed face. The old man didn't look up, just lifted and opened one gnarled hand. Hardin dropped the coin into it.

'Get yourself a cold drink, old man. This heat'll dry you out like a dead yucca.'

The Indian made no acknowledgement: Hardin had kept moving, anyway. As he crossed the street towards a diner, he didn't notice the big man with the craggy face, leaning against a saloon awning support, watching him with narrowed eyes.

The man unfolded his arms and reached into his vest pocket for the makings, the sun glinting off the tin star pinned to his shirt.

His name was Corey Flint, sheriff of Wildwood.

★　★　★

'The drifter's cheatin'! Son of a bitch is slippin' 'em in from the bottom of the deck!'

A stunned silence was abruptly broken as chairs scraped back hurriedly, at least one turning over, in the race to get away from the table with its scattered cards and piles of coins and notes making up the stake for the current hand.

Only two men remained at the table: the man with the slicked-back hair who had made the accusation, and Cole Hardin.

The man with the pomaded hair, dressed in a flowered vest over a silk shirt with baggy sleeves and grey, whipcord trousers, had a look of thunder on his face. His eyes were restless, raking the still seated Hardin up and down. The pearl shell butt of a pistol holstered under his left arm caught the lamplight and he worked his long fingers on both hands, opening and closing them vigorously.

Hardin scrubbed a hand around his stubbled jaw, cool grey eyes never leaving the gambler. 'You ain't wearing eyeglasses, amigo, and I reckon you'd need 'em set at about a hundred magnification and you still wouldn't've seen any deal from the bottom of my deck.'

Hardin stood slowly and the other man rose quickly, kicking irritably at his chair. It skidded away into the edge of the crowd that had gathered. He went by the name of Silk but his voice was far from smooth as he spoke. It was harsh with tension.

'Hardin, you made that full house too easy on a chance draw of two cards. Draw two and it means you already got three of a kind, but the odds of turnin' that into a full house don't bear thinkin' about! Unless you cheat!'

'Feller, name of Moose Hendriks, back in Wichita did a little study on that — heard of him?' Hardin was calm.

'Anyone's ever turned a pasteboard knows Moose is only the best card player in the country!' Silk curled a lip. 'But I'm talkin' to you, not Moose.'

Hardin held up his left hand in a pause sign. 'Moose figured it out that in draw poker — like we been playing — you can make a two-card draw to a single pair and a kicker card with a one in ten chance of improving the pair to four-of-a-kind . . . or a full house. One in ten — that's almost as good as making a three card draw, specially if the kicker card is high, ace or king.' He tapped his cards which lay fanned out face-up on the green tablecloth. 'I drew an ace of diamonds and a queen of spades. I already had two queens and my kicker card was an ace of clubs: full house.' Silk was frowning and Hardin smiled thinly. 'Course, it has bluff value, too — other players might figure I was already holding three-of-a-kind and drop out of the betting. Some kind of panic, start howlin' 'cheat' . . . sound like anyone you know, Silk?'

The gambler dragged down a deep breath, face flushing, and Hardin suspected Silk realized he had been bluffed, knew the other players would figure it out, too, and humiliation had driven him to make the wild accusation. Now he had to back it up — or eat crow.

His nostrils flared. 'Double talk!

Tryin' to dodge the issue! I *seen* you slip a card onto your pile! If that ain't cheating, I dunno what is!' He looked around wildly. 'And if you other fellers was in on that hand an' don't feel we gotta do somethin' about it, then . . . then you're yaller!'

The other players who had abandoned the table growled, and one short-assed cowboy, with a scarred, belligerent face, snapped, 'You better figure who you're fightin', feller!' He jerked a thumb towards Hardin. 'Him or me — and mebbe some others.'

Two of the card players nodded, grim-faced, but the third player remained expressionless.

He's stalling, Hardin thought. *But why . . . ?*

'Relax, Hank. His fight's with me.' Hardin walked around the table and Silk stepped back again, tensing, a hand going across his chest to rest close to the pearl-handled gun butt. Hardin took one long step forward and backhanded Silk across his narrow face.

The man fell sprawling over a nearby table, causing the men sitting there to leap to their feet, swearing, as the gambler's weight upset the table's balance. He crashed to the floor and struggled to get up. Hardin stood easy, with boots slightly spread, a couple of yards away.

'Silk, you're a damn liar and a sore loser. Admit it and eat some crow and we'll call it quits. But you get up and I'll kill you.'

Silk paused, a trickle of blood on his lips, hatred in his eyes. He moved as if to distribute his weight better, still sprawling, suddenly grabbed a chair and skidded it into Hardin. Cole was a shade late in dodging and it struck him in the hip, throwing his balance. He went down to one knee knocking over the card table, money and cards spilling. With a roar of triumph, Silk reared upright, lamplight flashing from the gun he whipped from the shoulder holster.

There was thunder in the big room

and Silk lifted to his toes, eyes flying wide as if they would pop from their sockets. His mouth worked at silent words and slowly his knees buckled and he sprawled on his face. His gun skidded in the wet sawdust to come to rest a couple of feet from one outstretched hand.

Cole Hardin straightened up, smoking sixgun still in his right hand, every eye in that saloon bar on him. He watched the motionless Silk for a few moments, then looked around at the men. 'Silk drew first. You all saw it.'

The silence dragged on for only a moment or two and then someone nodded and several agreed and then everyone was commenting: *Yeah, Silk reached for his gun first. Silk was way too slow! Should never've been fool enough to call Hardin a cheat. He's been askin' for trouble for a long time.*

It was clear all the sympathy was with Hardin. Men started forward, righting the overturned tables, the spilled money and cards trampled underfoot.

Hardin was collecting some of his winnings when Sheriff Corey Flint came slamming in through the batwings and demanded to know what in hell was going on in his town.

Everyone tried to tell him at once. Flint took off his hat, revealing thick wheat-coloured hair, dark with sweat. He slapped the hat several times hard against his upper thigh. Dust spurted and the noise, like muffled gunshots, brought silence to the room. He glared at Hardin.

'You drifted in this afternoon. Saw you talkin' with Ward Jericho. Seen you give that old Injun some money, too.'

Hardin nodded slightly. 'That'd be right.'

'Jericho's been in a lot of trouble with the law — you know that?'

Hardin hesitated. 'Never heard he was in a *lot* of trouble.'

Flint looked exasperated. 'Lot or little, if it's law trouble, it's *important* trouble, and if he's a friend of yours, and *you* get yourself in trouble with the law — well, let's go on down to my office and we'll talk about it.'

Under cover of his hat, Flint had slid his Colt from his belt holster and brought it into view now. He notched back the hammer. 'You gonna gimme an argument?'

Cole Hardin shook his head, aware the the crowd were just as startled as he was by the sheriff's action.

'Plenty of witnesses heard Silk call me a card cheat. I knew he was just being a sore loser so I gave him a chance to back down. Instead he went for his gun. Seems straightforward to me, Sheriff.'

Men started to tell the sheriff this was so, many voices overlapping. With a scowl, Flint fired a shot into the roof, bringing down a little plaster and piece of a splintered lath. He glared around at the now silent group. 'That's as maybe, but what I'm interested in is the timing of it.'

Hardin frowned. 'What's that mean?'

Flint swung his hard eyes back to the tall cowboy.

'Means your little fracas with Silk took place at exactly the same time as someone broke into the bank. Now, ain't that kind of coincidental? Me wonderin' which way I should go — check the gunfire or listen to Banker Borden screamin' in my ear that he's just had a nightwatchman slugged and was almost rid down himself while them robbers got away with a big haul? And Borden recognized one as your friend Jericho!'

The sheriff's face and voice hardened.

'Sounds to me like this fracas could've been a diversion that gave them bank robbers time to get away. No, don't say nothin' right now, Hardin! Just hand me your gun and come with me — or Silk's gonna have company on his way to hell.'

2

Thieves

After he had left Hardin that afternoon, Ward Jericho went to the Palace saloon and met three men in the bar: Hambone, Utah McCann and a sober, taciturn ranny who only used the name 'Kirk'.

They gathered around Jericho who signalled to the barkeep for beers and whiskeys all round. The hard liquor was tossed down dry throats pronto, the burning taste washed away with a mouthful of beer. No one spoke for a time and Jericho leaned his elbows on the bar edge, looked around and saw Silk standing by the tinny-sounding piano which was mercifully silent at the moment.

Jericho thumbed back his trail-worn

hat, tilted it over his left eye, then pushed it back again. All with his left hand.

Silk was toying with the buttons on his flowered vest and he nodded gently, turned away and disappeared through a narrow door that led to the back room.

'All fixed then?' asked Utah McCann, a dried-out *hombre* in worn clothes, his black vest frayed and food-stained. He sniffed hard, wiped the back of a hand over his large nostrils.

Kirk and Hambone, the latter a skinny streak of misery in his twenties, youngest of the quartet and sometimes referred to as 'The Dummy', looked expectantly at Jericho.

'All set,' he said slowly, signalling the barkeep for another round. 'Last drink till we're back in our hole-in-the-wall.'

Utah and Kirk looked some disappointed but Hambone grinned, showing buck teeth . . . some might say he looked a mite 'tetched' at times like this or when he imitated birds' calls.

They met just before seven that

night, behind the livery, and followed Jericho down a weed-grown path and along the edge of a dogleg creek where horses were already tethered to bushes. 'Watch 'em, Ham,' Jericho said.

The young man gasped in protest. 'Aw, heck, Jer, you said I could be in this one!'

'You are. You're in charge of the getaway broncs. That's your contribution. And mind that new one of mine!'

'Hell-damn! I wanted to be *in* it, you know? With you fellers, right in the thick of things.'

Jericho grinned, his teeth barely visible in the darkness. He clapped a hand to Hambone's shoulder. 'We need someone reliable to handle the broncs, Ham. We know you'll be where you're s'posed to be. You're reliable.'

The flattery worked, partially, anyway, and Hambone nodded, but muttered to himself. The others moved away, following Jericho away from the creek now. A square building blotted out the stars and they knew they were looking at the rear of the bank.

Jericho put out a hand, stopping them. They paused, heard the footsteps, and a few moments later saw the shadowy shape of the nightwatchman on his rounds, checking the rear of the building. Jericho waited till the man was rattling the padlock on the heavy rear door, then stepped forward, stumbling and weaving as he approached the startled watchman. The man spun around as Jericho slurred, 'Hey, feller — how in hell do I find my way back to the Palace? Judas, come out to take a leak an' guess I got somehow turned right aroun' — dunno where the hell I am . . . '

The nightwatchman, fairly heavy but in his sixties, dropped a hand to his gun butt. He cleared his throat, tried to sound hard: 'You're at the rear of the bank, mister, and that's right where you ain't s'posed to be!'

'The bank? Hell, I want the goddamn bar! I got no business with no *bank!*'

'I'll say you ain'. Now you get . . *Hey!*'

The word was choked off as Jericho's Colt cracked hard against the man's skull. It whipped back and forth across his shocked face, then bounced off his head a second time. He dropped like a felled steer in a slaughterhouse. Before he was still, Jericho was kneeling beside him, wrenching the ring of keys from the man's belt. Jericho stumbled, and swore, kicked the moaning body callously aside and fumbled for the keys. The one he wanted was fifth from the ring's belt clip. He found it, Utah beside him now, Kirk standing at the corner, pressed against the brickwork as he kept watch down the alley that led to Main.

In minutes, Jericho and Utah were inside and groping along the narrow passage that led to the employees' rooms and the offices. The big safe was in Banker Borden's office and he had the only key. *Or believed he did.* But long ago, Jericho had met a man in the

Territorial Prison where he was 'vacationing' briefly after 'mistakenly' taking a horse from the hitchrack that didn't belong to him. And this man had once worked for the company that had installed their make of safe in the Wildwood bank. He had managed to make a copy of the duplicate emergency key and Jericho, a man with an eye to the future, had offered a deal. The man was reluctant but after being fed some of the prison's potent moonshine let slip that he wore the key next to his skin night and day.

He met with a fatal accident not long after . . .

Now Jericho took that same duplicate copy from an inside pocket, unwrapped it from the creased waxed paper and slid it into the safe door lock.

It went in so smoothly he thought it wasn't going to work, but it engaged the tumblers when he twisted first right, then hard left — and moments later the money-laden shelves were exposed.

Utah had the bags ready, scooped the

paper money in with eager arms. They didn't bother with silver coins, they were only extra weight. But a few gold ones were dropped in amongst the bills. They were just about to close the door again when Jericho saw a leather valise that had two straps each with sealing wax over the buckles and flap lock.

'Must be somethin' valuable inside!' he said, snatching it up, and hurried after Utah, who wasn't waiting for anyone.

Hambone had the horses ready and they mounted fast, wheeled the animals and dug in the spurs — just as a fringed surrey pulled across the alley and a man Jericho recognized as Borden, the banker himself, jumped down.

'Hold it! Hold it, you damn thieves!'

He was brandishing a gun and at the same time there was a muffled gunshot that Jericho knew came from the Palace saloon. It startled the banker and he turned around sharply towards the sound. Jericho didn't hesitate: he spurred his mount forward, raking savagely, leaping it half its length. The banker heard the rattle of harness and the gusting protest of the horse, spun about and shouted in alarm with the mount almost on top of him.

He was hurled sideways as the big horse's shoulder struck him. Borden rolled under the surrey between the wheels. He had dropped his gun somewhere, groped wildly for it.

By the time Borden had crawled out from under the surrey the thieves had disappeared into the night along the creekbank. The banker, shaking and breathing hard, made another unsuccessful search for his pistol, staggered to the alley mouth in time to see Sheriff Flint starting to run towards the saloon from the direction of his office.

'Sheriff! Sheriff! Help me! The bank's been robbed . . . '

★　★　★

'So, like I said in the saloon, I had to make up my mind pronto where I went first, the bank or the saloon. I figured if there was gunfire someone could've been shot, so . . . '

He spread his hands, leaning back in his desk chair, hard eyes glinting in the lamplight as he watched Hardin seated across the desk from him.

'And I was right, wasn't I? Poor old Silk had been dealt his last hand.'

'I hear he made a habit of picking on strangers he lost money to at cards,' Cole Hardin said.

Flint shrugged. 'Silk was kinda tetchy. He could bluff most times .. but not you, eh?'

'Look, Sheriff, everyone in that saloon heard him call me a cheat. And heard me give him a chance to back off. He went for his gun first.'

'I know all that!' Flint snapped. 'It could be just the way you say, but *it happened just at the right time to divert me from the bank bein' robbed!* It was all a set-up.'

'Hell, I never met Silk before tonight.'

'No, but you know Ward Jericho. And Banker Borden recognized him as one of the robbers.'

'This afternoon was the first time I'd seen Jericho in nearly four years. We both worked for the same stageline, as shotgun guards, at one time.'

Flint studied Hardin's face soberly. 'What'd you talk about today?'

'Just the last time we met when we threw a wingding.'

Flint sighed, then took out a sack of tobacco and rolled a cigarette. He pushed the makings across the desk and soon both men were smoking. 'You have to kill Silk?'

'He went for his gun. He was gonna bust a cap on me.'

'We-ell, I got no dodgers on you. Make it my business to find out the name of fellers who come to town and then I go through my papers. But I've heard your name before.'

'Hardin's not an uncommon one.'

'Hardin, mebbe, but Cole Hardin is a specific person. You a trail man as well as shotgun guard?'

'I'm anything that'll pay an honest dollar, Sheriff, cowman, bronc-buster, miner, shotgun guard, stage driver — up to six-in-hand — river ferryman, and a dozen other things including a deputy sheriff under Matt Cohan in Denver ... I'm a drifter. One day pretty soon I guess I'll settle down. Getting on towards forty now so it's about time.'

Flint nodded, lifted his hard eyes. 'But you're not settlin' down around here.'

It was a flat statement and Hardin returned the steely gaze. 'Wasn't aiming to, but I'll move along come daylight if it'll keep you happy.'

'I'll decide when you move along. For tonight, you're my guest.' Flint smiled thinly, gesturing to the door that obviously led to the cell block.

Hardin straightened in the chair. 'Now wait a minute! You've got nothing to lock me up for!'

'Well, that's somethin' I'll decide, too

— Gotta look into Silk's death some more and I want you where I can reach you . . . and that guard ain't too chipper. Maybe I'll send a wire to Matt Cohan. See if he remembers you.'

Flint already had Hardin's gun and he stood now, a hand on the butt of his own holstered Colt, the other reaching down for a set of keys on a heavy iron ring.

'Do it easy or do it hard — I'll allow you to make *that* decision!'

Hardin swore softly and stood up. 'Matt'll remember me, but listen — that palomino horse you saw Jericho and me admiring is mine now. I won it in that card game.'

'The hell you say! That belonged to Silk. He won it off a rancher couple weeks back. Cheated, I s'pect.'

'He put it up as stakes, his hand against mine, but I drew to a pair and a kicker and made a full house, which is what started the fracas. He never thought he'd lose the horse but it's mine now, and I want to see it stabled properly for the night.'

Flint jerked his head towards the cellblock door. 'Just come on through to your bedroom, Hardin. Don't worry about nothin' else.'

'That's a valuable horse and — '

'Yeah, it is — and your friend Jericho was ridin' it when he quit the bank. C'mon, let's go. I want my supper.'

* * *

Hardin took a long time to get to sleep in the cell. He was not a total stranger to jails and the thin straw mattress was no worse nor better than others he'd found across the country in his travels. He had tobacco and he smoked a cigarette, sitting on the bunk with his back against the wall.

It was possible that Jericho had set up the card game deal with Silk if, as Flint maintained, they knew each other. Of course, no one would have figured it would escalate into a gunfight. If Silk had done this kind of thing before, challenging the winning hand when he was short of cash — and even had to stake his fine horse in a bid to stay in the game — it was likely that most men would back off when he reached for his gun.

But Hardin was fast, reacted instinctively. He had been top payroll guard on several stagelines and Ward Jericho would know this. *But would the man have deliberately set Silk against him, with the chance the gambler might get shot and killed?*

The answer was 'yes' and Hardin didn't have to think about it for more than a few seconds. Jericho had the reputation of being quick on the trigger, had killed three or four would-be road agents trying to stop stages he was guarding. One was a kid no more than sixteen. Hardin knew Jericho had been given harsh warnings by lawmen for shooting first and talking later.

Well, it depended on how well Jericho knew Silk and whether he had a grudge to square away. Or, if Jericho had badly wanted something Silk had, like that palomino!

Yeah, from what he knew of Ward Jericho, it was possible — probable — that he had set it up with the notion of getting Silk killed by Hardin. It wouldn't be certain but if it came down to real gunplay the odds were in favour of it happening. Jericho knew Hardin's reputation as a fast gun.

He swore softly and ground out his fifth cigarette, mouth dry and foul from too much tobacco. Damn! He hated being used! The thing now of course was he had to convince Corey Flint he wasn't in any kind of a deal with Jericho.

And once he had done that and — hopefully — Flint had turned him loose, he would get on Jericho's trail.

He didn't care about the bank money.

But he damn well wanted that palomino.

*   *   *

Sheriff Flint was almost home after stopping at the telegraph office and sending his wire to Matt Cohan. He paused to light another cigarette and heard the footsteps behind him coming up fast. He dropped the still burning match and spun, right hand dropping to gun butt. He checked his draw halfway when he recognized the hurrying, hard-breathing shadow behind him as Banker Harrison Borden.

'Why the . . . hell you . . . have to walk . . . so damn fast?'

'I'm hungry,' Flint said. 'What's your hurry? Ain't nothin' more we can do about the robbery till daylight now.'

Borden mopped his sweating face with a large handkerchief, wheezed and coughed some, then said, 'Well, we better do something — as quickly as possible.'

Flint frowned. 'Why? How much they get away with?'

'Only about four thousand, near as, dammit.'

'Nothin' to tear up the countryside

over in the middle of the night.'

Borden, breathing easier now, looked steadily at the lawman, their faces pale and greyish in the dim light from lamps burning under shopfront awnings close by.

'Four thousand dollars — and Macauley's valise!'

Flint actually dropped the newly-lit cigarette at the banker's words. Something like a hand closed around his heart. 'What the hell was that doin' in your safe?'

'Mac sent it down by special messenger this afternoon. He's on his way here with The Major but, having to travel mostly by stagecoach across lonely country, he didn't want to risk a hold-up. There've been a lot lately.'

'I blame well know! Some of 'em have been in my bailiwick. But, Jesus, couldn't you've told me you had the goddamn valise?'

'Why? Do you have a safer place than my bank vault to keep it?'

Flint snorted. 'My bottom desk

drawer with the busted lock would've been safer than your goddamn vault!'

Borden sighed. 'Yes, well, it was rotten luck that Jericho robbed the safe tonight. Tomorrow, Mac ought to be here by then, with The Major. We'll have to tell him.'

The sheriff shook his head several times. 'Aw, no. You tell him. I won't be here when he arrives. I'll be out lookin' for the thieves! Doin' my job.'

'I always knew I could count on you when the chips were down, Corey!' he said bitterly.

Flint shrugged. 'My supper's gettin' cold. You be sure to tell Mac where I am when he gets here . . . '

'Wait a minute!'

Flint scowled. 'Come on! Hurry it up!'

'You have a suspect in your cells, a man you figure could've been in it with Jericho.' Borden pushed on swiftly. 'If your man was in on the deal, he'll know where they went . . . ' The banker let the words trail off. He could just make out the sheriff's face and saw that the man savvied what he was saying. 'Remember The Major's coming with Macauley — '

'Leave it with me,' Flint said curtly, turned and continued on his way.

Borden seemed a lot happier now as he turned and walked in the opposite direction.

3

Trails

It was pitch dark when Hardin's light sleep was disturbed by the rattle of a key in the lock of the cell door.

He blinked, turned his head and saw the glow of a couple of lanterns. The amber light showed three or four men. The only one he recognized as he sat up quickly and swung his legs over the side of the bunk was Corey Flint. The sheriff swung the barred door back and stepped inside, followed by two hulking men.

Hardin, still sitting on the bunk, tensely now, watched them warily. Big men, beefy shoulders, hamfisted, one with a battered face, the other looking pleasant enough, except for his eyes. They were watching Harden without much expression. As far as the big man was concerned, Hardin was no more interesting than the cockroach that scuttled away beneath the bunk.

That was when he knew he was in trouble and started to stand up: he'd run across this kind of thing before. *Hired help from the gutters or the back alleys where drunks could be rolled easily and rarely fought back . . .*

The one with the battered face was already cracking his knuckles, staring open-mouthed, looking forward to whatever was to come next.

Hardin found out fast enough what that was.

Flint said nothing, holding a lantern, the other one set down by the end of the bunk. He stepped outside, pulling the door closed after him, holding it in place by the bars.

The man with the pleasant face and sandy hair feinted with a sudden left and swung a right that would've taken Hardin's head off — if he had been fool enough to put his head in the way. But he simply slid off the side of the bunk onto his knees and the fist whistled over his head and the sandy-haired man stumbled one step forward.

Too bad for Sandy — it put him in a perfect position for Hardin's right fist to come up like a hunting hawk and bury itself deep in Sandy's groin. The man gave a choked scream, clawed at himself as his legs folded. Hardin dived sideways as the other hardcase swung a boot. It caught his shoulder, spinning him, and he went with the spin, using its impetus to skid across the floor between the grovelling, choking Sandy and the other man who was just now regaining his balance from the hard kick.

Hardin twisted onto his back, grabbed the man's boot, yanked savagely, and brought an alarmed cry from the man. He crashed into his companion who was moaning as he rocked back and forth on his hams. They fell in a heap and Flint shouted something. Hardin kicked with both boots indiscriminately, hitting the sandy-haired one in the head, knocking him full-length. He tried to kick the other, too, but the man was tough, fended off the boot, and grabbed Hardin's leg with both big hands and heaved to his feet, lifting.

He hauled powerfully and spun, hurling Hardin across the cell to crash into the far wall. The drifter saw stars and planets and galaxies, and just had enough sense left to draw up his knees to his chest and huddle into a ball where the wall joined the floor.

The big man, blood streaming from his nose and smearing his mouth, wiped the back of a hand across his face, moved in fast and began kicking wildly. Hardin's body shuddered and twisted and the jolting pain dragged a reddish curtain over his eyes, blurring his vision. He was moving entirely by instinct now, straightening out of his crouch, launching himself flat-bodied along the floor. One kick missed but came close enough to pick up a loose fold of his shirt and rip the cloth. The big man was off balance and as he fought to find equilibrium Hardin clawed his way erect. He had to pause, find the strength to heave off the wall. A large fist drove into his kidneys and he felt his gorge rise as the searing pain coursed through him. His legs buckled and as the man came in with one fist drawn back over his shoulder, Hardin managed to get a boot against the wall and propel himself forward. He ducked under the fist as it whistled by, pummelled at the man's rock-hard midriff, snapped his head up as he felt the other body sagging a little. His timing was good: just as the man's face came down, Hardin's head came up — fast and with his body weight behind it.

There were crunching sounds, half-smothered grunts, and then the big body stumbled along the wall, arms flung wide. Hardin, fighting for breath, unsteady on his feet, went after him, aching arms ready to pummel and maim. He saw movement out in the passage but it was blurred, without detail. He hooked a blow into his quarry, drew back for another and — There was a sensation like the roof caving-in on him and that was all he remembered for some time . . .

He was back on the bunk when he came round, slowly, painfully, nostrils clogged with congealing blood, every bone in his body aching as if a horse had rolled on him. The back of his head had a tender knot on it the size of a hen egg.

They stood in a small semi-circle now, watching him. The lamps were turned up and there was more light in the cell and the smell of hot coal oil. Something glinted and when he opened his good eye a little more he saw it was Flint's sheriff's star.

'Don't think it's over, Hardin,' the sheriff said.

The man whose face he had ruined with the headbutt said, 'Hell, I ain't even started yet on the bastard!'

'Easy, Grady, you may yet get your chance. You too, Ridge.' This last was directed at the sandy-haired man who was leaning against the wall, massaging his groin area very carefully.

'Just gimme five minutes alone with the son of a bitch,' Ridge gritted. 'Just five, Sher'ff.'

Flint lifted a hand. 'We'll see.' He took a folded and creased yellow oblong of paper from his shirt pocket. Hardin recognized it as a telegraph form as Flint waved it in front of his battered face. 'This is what saved you, mister. Just delivered from Matt Cohan. Seems he thinks you're a man to ride the river with, wants you to know if ever you need a job he'll take you on as his deputy again, and pay double.'

Hardin still had most of his winnings from the card game: some of the money had disappeared when it was being 'retrieved' from the saloon floor after the shooting, but he still had a good wad. Flint had locked it away in his desk drawer, even gave him a receipt for it. He didn't feel like working the helltowns again, with Matt Cohan or anyone else.

'I'll pass,' he said, his voice thick.

'Makes no difference,' Flint said, pocketing the yellow form again. 'Thing is if Cohan thinks enough of you to want to hire you again, I guess it means you're OK. But it don't mean you couldn't've stepped across the line to Jericho's side of the law since you last seen Cohan.'

'Well, you'll have to take my word on that.' Hardin winced. *Man, his ribs felt all caved-in. His head seemed to be two sizes too big. His jaw felt as if it was skewed halfway around his face.* 'Why the hell you set these mangy bears on me?'

Grady and Ridge both growled and started forward but Flint held them back, not looking at them. His gaze was steady on Hardin. 'Thought you might be able to tell me where Jericho's hideout is. Figured a man like you would need a mite of softenin' up first.'

'What? Judas, didn't you listen to

anything I said? Today — yesterday, was the first time I'd seen Jericho in nigh on four years. Sure, I knew he'd pulled a few stage hold-ups and so on but I *heard* or read about 'em. I wasn't in on anything outside the law, with or without him.'

'Sounds like we got Mr Goody-Goody here, Sheriff,' said Grady, dabbing at his swollen nose and smashed mouth.

Flint looked dubious. Thing was, he knew a man like Matt Cohan wouldn't stand up for anyone he didn't think was worth it. He was a well-respected lawman, carried a lot of weight in many circles. Flint was a reasonably honest lawman, though if he saw a chance to make a fast buck without exerting himself too much, he would grab with both hands. Like this deal he was in with Borden right now. And he didn't want anything to go wrong there. He had learned long ago to look out for Number One.

The fact he had turned Grady and

Ridge loose on Hardin — although it hadn't been successful — would be in his favour when Macauley arrived with that cold-livered bastard who called himself The Major. Hell! He didn't have to do anything else! Just turn Cole Hardin loose, let him lead the way to Jericho if he was in on the bank deal. If not, well, not much harm done; more done to his two hardcases.

'All right, Hardin, Matt Cohan's word will just have to be good enough. Forget the roughin' up.' He smiled crookedly and threw a mocking glance at his bloody sidekicks. 'Now you boys leave Hardin be, you savvy? We made a mistake is all . . .'

'We made a mistake?' growled Ridge. 'You made it but we suffered for it.'

'You'll get your money just the same. Now clear out. I know where to find you next time I need you.'

Grady looked at Hardin. 'Make it a long time,' he said on the way out.

Hardin started for the door but Flint closed it in his face. 'Hey, what the hell?

I thought you said — '

'Said Matt Cohan's word was good enough for me, but you stay put for now. I know where you'll be come mornin' that way. I'll get you some water to wash-up in and some iodine, even a cup of coffee with a slug of whiskey in it. But you're stayin' put in the cell overnight!'

Hardin was too tired, and had too bad a headache from where the sheriff had slugged him, to argue further. The sooner it was daylight and he shook the dust of this lousy town the better.

But he wasn't leaving this country without that palomino.

★ ★ ★

The sheriff even brought him breakfast on a tray: eggs, bacon, a dollop of fried-over potatoes, coffee. It wasn't high-class fare but Hardin appreciated the gesture. When he was finished and stood up by his bunk, ready to leave, the lawman handed him a sack of

47

tobacco and papers.

'Guess I went overboard last night, but the Banker's in a blue fit over the robbery, and he put a burr under me.'

Hardin fired-up the cigarette he had made, careful of his cut and swollen lips. He blew smoke, looking coolly at Flint. 'Suppose you'd slam the door and lock it again if I took a poke at you.'

Flint smiled wryly. 'We-ell, I wouldn't recommend you try it, even if I understand your motive.'

Hardin jammed his hat on and swore softly: that bump where Flint had slugged him was mighty tender. 'I'll get my money and then my gear from the rooming house and be on my way. I doubt that I'll be heading back this way again.'

'That could be a good move.'

Their gazes locked. 'You're a mistrustful son of a bitch, Flint, aren't you?'

The sheriff stiffened, stood back, holding the door wide, and jerked his head down the passage. 'Don't push your luck, mister.'

Hardin moved stiffly, got his sixgun from the front office, and was amused to find that Flint had unloaded it.

'Keep it that way till you clear town.'

'Like I said, Sheriff. You need to put more trust in your fellow man.'

Flint said nothing and handed over the money from his drawer, demanding that Hardin sign for it. Afterwards, Hardin moved out, collected his warbag, rifle and bedroll from the rooming house and settled his small bill there. He walked back to the livery and down to the stall where his old paint gelding stood munching on some straw. He patted its muzzle, took a handful of the straw and rubbed down the coarse coat, surprised to see the old Indian he had given a half-dollar sweeping out some of the stalls. Making tobacco money, he thought.

He had the paint saddled and was leading it out of the stall when suddenly the Indian was standing in front of him, hard-haired broom in hand. He nodded briefly to Hardin.

'Morning, Chief,' Hardin said and went to step around the old man. But the Indian didn't move, set his milky grey eyes on Hardin's face. He gestured with an eagle-talon hand, turned and walked down to a small corral just outside a wide side door. Curious, Hardin followed, leaving the paint's reins trailing.

The Indian leaned on the pole rails, pointing to the ground; there were hoofmarks there, many of them, but the old man used his broom handle to touch just three amongst the others. 'Palomino,' he said in a phlegmy voice.

Hardin frowned as he looked at him. 'Yeah?'

'You know what track to look for now.'

Hardin nodded, smiling crookedly. 'Why, thanks, Chief. I'm much obliged.'

'Cold beer good.'

'I didn't think they'd serve you.'

The man showed him some pinkish

gums. 'Know way.'

Hardin chuckled and swung aboard the paint, touching a hand briefly to his hatbrim. He started to fumble out another coin but the Indian shook his head, the silver grey strands flapping briefly across his walnut face.

'No. Name Hee-cha. The owl.'

'That's Lakota, isn't it? You're a long way from home, Chi — er — Hee-cha.'

'Long way. Never chief, but.'

Well, you'd've made a good one, thought Hardin: the old man was stooped now but would have been tall in his youth and the frame was still large, though long since devoid of the muscle and sinew he would have known in his marauding days on the warpath.

'Well, *adios*, Hee-cha. Obliged again for your help.'

The old man lifted a hand briefly and watched Hardin ride out of the yard, turn across a vacant lot and then back towards Main. He would clear town in a few minutes.

Hee-cha returned to his sweeping

and a few minutes later saw Sheriff Flint come out of the stable owner's small office. He paused in his sweeping as the lawman came towards him.

'Get yourself a horse. I want you as a tracker on my posse.'

'Work Mr Todd.' The old man pointed towards the livery owner standing in the narrow doorway of his office cubicle.

'Says he works for you, Todd.'

'Some might call it work,' called Todd with a crooked grin. 'It's OK, Crazy Hoss, you go with the sheriff . . . Your job'll still be here when you get back.'

Hee-cha hesitated and Flint impatiently wrenched the broom from the old fingers and flung it down the aisle.

'C'mon, we ain't got all day.'

The Indian rubbed his gnarled fingers and nodded, moving slowly down the line of stalls to where a wide-chested grulla stood at the feed bin.

'You sure he can see well enough to track, Todd?' Flint asked sardonically.

'Mebbe. Can always put a collar and a leash on him, get him down on all fours so's he's closer to the ground.'

Flint chuckled. 'Be handy if I wanted to kick him in the backside,' he allowed, and Todd laughed.

Then the old man came out of the stall leading the grulla and Flint stalked away, snapping at him to get a move on. Just outside the wide main doors of the livery, the hastily convened posse waited. Eight men, all armed and looking grim. There were no volunteers here.

Flint had Hee-cha range alongside him and then led the posse down Main where folk on the walk could see. Some waved, most just stared, thankful the tough sheriff hadn't called on them to join him.

'Not lookin' for Jericho's tracks, Chief,' Flint told the old man who lifted his eyes to the sheriff's face, waiting patiently for the lawman to continue. 'No. You just follow the tracks made by that drifter. He'll lead us to the others if

I ain't mistaken.'

The old Indian said nothing and his expression, as always, was unreadable. So Flint wondered why the hell the oldster made him feel like he was being laughed at . . . ?

★　★　★

The four bank robbers had slept the sleep of men with clear consciences — or, leastways, with consciences that didn't bother them.

They were in their hole-in-the-wall, in Flatiron Canyon country, high up in the sawtooth ranges that marched along the horizon. Having used this place successfully before and for quite some time without discovery, they were confident they were safe here. Jericho hadn't even set a guard, though that would change. He told Hambone he had first lookout after breakfast. The young outlaw shrugged: he didn't care. He could make himself comfortable amongst the rocks and get in some extra sleep. He reckoned no posse would find them in this tangle of hills.

They had counted the money and it had come out at a little more than four thousand. Jericho allotted $750 to each of his men and kept the rest as his share. No one complained: Jericho was the brains of this outfit.

'Now, let's see if we've got ourselves a bonus,' he said, drawing the leather valise to him.

He examined it, turning it in his hands, shook it against his ear. There was sealing wax on each of the leather strap fastenings and it was this that had made him think there might be some valuables inside.

'Din't hear it rattle when you shook it,' Utah McCann allowed.

'No. Could be jewels in a chamois roll or somethin',' Jericho said hopefully, looking at Kirk. 'What you think, Kirk?'

'Think we best open it and make sure.'

Jericho nodded, his gaze lingering a

shade on the taciturn man. He never had much liked Kirk's way of speaking. The man said little but when he spoke he made it sound like he knew more than you, was smarter, and only tolerated the company because he had no choice.

Jericho took out his clasp knife, opened the big blade and chipped at the sealing wax, but grew impatient and ended cutting the binding straps. He mangled the brass lockplates and prised open the flimsy locks, threw back the flap, eagerly looking inside. He swore.

'Aw, shoot! Nothin' but damn papers!' he growled, rummaging, pulling out handfuls of papers and tossing them on to the ground.

'Can use 'em to light the fire easy, Jer,' said Hambone helpfully.

Kirk picked up some of the handwritten papers, saw they were smeared grey with the writing in places barely visible because the grey had become almost black.

'Dirty, ain't they?' opined McCann.

'These've been photographed onto a glass plate then printed on the paper,' Kirk said slowly, examining as he spoke. 'They've got a legal look to them. There's a picture of a seal on some. Hey, I can read the heading: *Confidential.*'

'They ain't cash or jewellery,' growled Jericho, disappointed. 'Do what you like with 'em.'

'Might be worth something.'

'How would you know?' Jericho was irritable now, in a bad mood, flung the valise into some rocks near the smouldering campfire.

'If someone took the trouble to photograph them, I'd say these were stolen. The originals left in place . . . yeah, it's written in legal jargon, all right . . . '

'You read that stuff?' Jericho asked.

'Used to,' Kirk said, and he looked up to see Jericho snapping up his head to stare at him. Utah McCann frowned vacantly, just watching. 'I was a lawyer once.'

Jericho stared harder. 'You . . . ? A damn lawyer?'

'Well, sort of. Never actually got my papers. But studied for a few years, helped with a couple of court cases.'

'Well, I'll be damned. Why you never told me before?'

'Why? Would it make any difference to the way I hold up stages or rob banks?'

There he went again! That smart-talk, the fast back-answer. Well, if he had been a lawyer maybe that would explain it . . .

Aloud, Jericho said, 'I ain't sure. Why're you ridin' with us? Hankerin' to see both sides of the law?'

Kirk almost smiled. 'You're close, Jericho. Close.'

They waited but he didn't explain further. He had gathered all the papers from the valise now, stood and recovered the satchel itself, stuffing the papers inside.

'I'll look 'em over, see if we can use 'em.'

Jericho snorted. 'Use 'em to wipe your ass for all I care,' he said, still burning from his disappointment.

'How long we gonna stay here?' Utah asked.

Jericho rounded on him. 'Long as I say!'

'I know that — but how long is it?'

'Christ! Has everyone gotta be a smart-mouth! Goddamnit, just do like I say. We got us a good hideyhole here and mebbe we'll work out of it for a spell before movin' on. Lots of stages come out this way.'

'Railroad's coming, too,' Kirk said, putting in his two cents' worth. 'Be better and bigger pickings then.'

'Bigger risks, too,' Jericho said sourly. 'The express cars are full of shotgun guards.'

'Might be a way around that.'

Jericho frowned at Kirk. 'Yeah, there might be — and I'm workin' on it. You got some ideas, I want to hear 'em.'

'I haven't any ideas yet, Ward, but

there's gotta be some way around the guards.'

Jericho stood impatiently. 'Well, I'll let you know when I figure it out, OK?'

Kirk merely lifted a finger in acknowledgement.

Jericho scowled, turned on Hambone. 'The hell're you still sittin' around here for? Get up to that damn lookout!'

The young outlaw shrugged and got lazily to his feet, leaning down to pick up his rifle.

'OK, OK, Ward. I'm on my way.'

'An' don't go sleepin' on the job!' Jericho snapped, determined to have the last word. 'Or I'll shoot your pecker off — if I could find it!'

Hambone's lower lip protruded sullenly, hurt by Jericho's words.

And that was why Jericho had said them: he could be a mean bastard when he wanted.

4

Twisted Trails

Thanks to the old Indian showing him the kind of tracks made by the palomino, Hardin was able to follow the trail taken by Jericho and his outlaws.

It led through rock-studded brush country and into the foothills. The outlaws hadn't taken much trouble to cover their tracks — up till now. Then abruptly it became harder to find sign.

He dismounted, leading his weary paint, kneeling, lying full-length in an attempt to get the lowest angle possible where light might cast a small shadow, indicating a hoofprint. He thought he had a direction once and got too confident, figuring the way the sign pointed had to lead into a dry wash. So he rode there fast and dismounted again — and spent a half hour without finding even a lizard track.

Hat back off his forehead, rolling a cigarette, he stood hipshot and slowly looked around. The wash led nowhere, just to a crumbling earthen wall. So, he had been wrong and they had skirted the wash, likely knowing it was a dead-end. So where else could they go . . . ? He delayed lighting up, knowing the flare of a match would spoil his vision just a little — and that little might be all he needed to see something that would give him the clue he wanted.

But there was only the obvious: up to the high country. And there were miles of slopes lifting into the snow-capped sawtooth, well-timbered, affording good cover for many miles, all along the crests.

Well, that was it, all right. They had to be up there somewhere. When he had been deputy with Matt Cohan, Jericho had been a member of a gang who had robbed an express company.

They had run into the sierras and it had taken days to pick up a trail and had ended in a shoot-out high on the slopes. Jericho and two others had gotten away by sacrificing the other three gang members. Later, long after he had quit being a lawman, Hardin had heard man-bones had been found in a deep ravine below the twisting trail the fleeing outlaws must have taken. No sign of their horses but bullets had been found rattling on the ground under the ribcages of both skeletons. Someone had a strong sense of self-preservation.

Next thing he knew Jericho had turned up as a shotgun guard on the stageline — a loner, he claimed.

But he seemed to have a liking for high country and Hardin knew he had a chore ahead of him if Jericho had run to the snowline up there.

Not long after he found another track — unmistakably left by the palomino.

He mounted and rode with his rifle across his thighs, edging up slowly through the timber, tensed and waiting for the ambush shot that he mightn't even hear before the bullet slammed into him.

* * *

'Whoa! Where the hell you takin' us, damn you?'

Corey Flint hauled rein and yelled at Hee-cha. The old Indian slowed his grulla, turned creakingly in the saddle and looked at the lawman, puzzled.

'Don't gimme that innocent look, you stinkin' old coot! You know what you're doin' and I've only just figured it out!'

The Indian still seemed puzzled and gestured ahead and slightly left. 'Go this way.'

'We *don't* go that way!' Flint roared. He looked around at the sweating, begrimed posse men. 'This son of a bitch is leadin' us all over the countryside! Just recollected Hardin gave him a handout yesterday, and he was talkin' with him in the livery before he left town. I reckon old Owly here has been leadin' us astray, an' on purpose.'

'Because Hardin gave him a few cents?' asked one of the posse men, scoffing. 'I ain't never knowed an Injun who was grateful for nothin' a white-man ever give him.'

'Mebbe that's because you ain't never seen a white man give an Injun nothin' but a kick in the butt!' someone said, and got a small laugh from the others.

'Or a bullet, turnin' him into the only good kinda Injun,' said another surlily. 'I ain't been happy followin' this old cuss right from the start. You tried a shortcut, Sheriff, an' it din't work. Admit it.'

Flint knew the man was right and felt his ears burning and his cheeks colouring. He hated to be found out in his mistakes.

'No! Old Owly's the one made the mistake! If he'd done like I said, we'd be close to Jericho by now! I checked up on Hardin some and he used to be a scout and tracker up at Fort Sheldon when they had all that Injun trouble. Gave him some kinda medal he was so good. If we'd followed his trail, he'd've led us to Jericho, all right — I'd bet he knows where the bastard's holed-up, anyways. Even if he don't, he wants that palomino bad an' he'd bust his back lookin'.'

'Where'd he go?' a man said suddenly, loudly, and Flint, frowning, turned towards him.

'How the hell do I know? That's what I wanted old Owly for, to trail him . . .'

'No! Not Hardin!' the townsman said. 'Where the hell'd the Injun go?'

Bewilderedly, they looked around. There was no sign of Hee-cha, but the brush was moving slightly close to where he had halted his horse some yards ahead of the posse. And while Flint had been haranguing them, Owl had taken the opportunity and . . . disappeared.

Flint roared a curse, spurred his horse into the brush that was now settling back into place. He snatched up his rifle and levered three or four shots, raking the brush ahead, bullets whining off saplings.

'Well, that's the end of this posse, thank Christ!' said the man who had just noticed Hee-cha's disappearance. 'If Jericho's anywhere within a mile of here he'd hear that shootin'.'

'Hardin, too,' another man allowed.

A third stood in stirrups, shading his eyes. 'Hey, Sheriff! We're turnin' back! Ain't no use now!'

The posse members were eager to go back: they had been suffering for long hours in this heat for no profit. They were part-way down the slope when Sheriff Flint rode after them, smoking rifle in one hand, face purple with anger.

'Come back here, goddamn you! We ain't givin' up yet!'

'We already did,' someone called back and they all spurred their mounts on harder, down the slope.

Flint lifted the rifle and levered in a shell and with his finger curled round the trigger, suddenly swore and lowered the hammer.

He'd have to watch that temper of his! The short fuse he'd always had seemed to have grown even shorter with the passing years.

'Aw, hell! They're likely right. But I'd sure like to get my hands on that stinkin' old polecat of an Injun!'

He rode after the disappearing posse and felt the gradual knotting in his belly tighten appreciably.

He had just remembered that Borden had said Macauley and The Major would be arriving this afternoon.

He would have to face them when he got back to town and he didn't have one damn piece of good news for them.

★ ★ ★

Hardin swung sharply, right hand palming up his sixgun as he heard a horse pushing through brush to his left. He relaxed and released a breath as he recognized old Hee-cha. 'I damn near shot you, old man!'

The Indian showed him his pink gums. 'Everyone want to shoot me today.'

'Them shots I heard across on the other slope — someone using you for target practice?'

'Flint — not like where I lead him.'

'Using you as a tracker, was he? And you led him away from my trail . . . ? Or did you pick up Jericho's?'

'Flint wanted follow you. He think you know where Jericho went.'

Hardin shook his head slowly. 'He takes some convincing, that damn sheriff. Obliged to you again, Hee-cha. But you didn't have to risk your neck for me.'

The Owl shrugged bony shoulders. 'You want find Jericho?'

'Want my palomino.'

The Indian nodded. 'We find.'

'Listen, aren't you in enough trouble? Flint won't give up just 'cause you rode off.'

The gums again. 'No, posse give up.'

Hardin smiled. 'Poor old Flint. Your

name and mine ain't gonna be worth a plugged nickel from now on.'

Hee-cha pointed across the slope. 'See broken branch.'

Hardin hipped in his saddle and had to stare mighty hard before he saw a small speck of white against the green. 'How come you got eyes like that, Owl, when you had to squint so hard to see what I'd put in your hand yesterday?'

'Close not so good. Far, I see.'

So they rode across and sure enough there was a branch no thicker than Hardin's little finger on a bush, bent and snapped, the bark lifting a little to leave a dime-sized piece of white wood showing. He knew by the way it hung which way the horse that broke the twig was heading.

'So I was right, thinking he'd head for the high country.'

'Give good look.'

'Yeah. There could be shooting, Owl.'

The Indian grunted, urged his grulla past Hardin and angled more to the right, but still travelling upwards. When

Hardin rode up alongside, the Indian had dismounted and moved a few dead leaves aside, revealing a partial hoofprint. Hardin had to dismount and drop to one knee before he made out the distinctive deep left-hand nudge in the soil that identified the palomino's worn shoe on his left forefoot.

He stood and looked up the steepening slope.

'We might be caught on this mountain come dark,' Hardin opined aloud. 'Long way up there and few tracks.'

'Enough.' Hee-cha was already pointing upslope to another sign he had spotted. 'We go up, all way, then look again.'

The drifter nodded, remounting. Yes, it was the best way and would save time. He was glad he had the old Indian with him.

★   ★   ★

Corey Flint kind of wished he was still on the mountain slopes, cussing out that double-crossing Indian right then, too.

But he was in Borden's office and the banker sat behind his desk, grey-faced, sweating, one hand tending to twitch so that he covered it with the other to hide it. Flint's mouth felt dry as a dead dog's. Hell, he wished he hadn't thought of that simile! Nor anything with the word 'dead' in it! Not right now, the way things were.

There were two other men in the office. One was dressed in a brown pinstriped suit, the frock coat still a little dusty on the shoulders from the long stage coach ride down to Wild-wood. The other's clothes were dusty, too, dark grey shirt with fancy silver, spring-loaded armbands holding the loose folds of the sleeves so the cuff edges were exactly level with his wrist bones. His black whipcord trousers and black half-boots showed even more dust.

But the black leather gunrig around his waist, the holster on his right thigh, was free of all dust and the brass cartridges in the loops shone brightly. The gun itself was cleanest of all, what showed of it, the butt smooth and shiny from a lot of handling. He was a rangy man, medium tall, with a narrow, not-unhandsome face, although the eyes showed latent cruelty not far below the surface. There was an army campaign hat with a curled brim set squarely on his head, a leather thong knotted behind a pair of acorns for a band.

This was The Major, which made the man in the pinstripe suit, Macauley. He was not much over five feet three, his skin reflecting the good living he was accustomed to. *His* face was oval, mean and calculating, common to some ruthless businessmen. He raked mean eyes from Flint to Borden and back again to the sheriff.

'Get another posse and go back out there, and find this bastard you allowed to steal my valise!'

Flint swallowed. 'It was in Borden's

safe, Mac — I — I didn't even know it was here! He never told me!'

'Fewer that knew the better, I figured,' Borden said harshly, hoping it was the right thing to say.

'You're both fools,' Macauley said flatly. 'And you'll both be dead fools if that valise is not recovered quickly.'

'What — what was in it that's so — important, Mac?' Flint asked, feeling he had a right to know that much.

'I thought I told you to take a posse out and get looking?'

'Well, it's gonna be dark in an hour . . . '

'Don't waste that hour,' The Major said quietly.

Flint nodded. 'OK, but I — I just wondered what was so — '

'Papers,' snapped Macauley. 'Papers I am not supposed to possess! If my — employers learn I have had them copied, well, let's not go into *that*! It cost me a small fortune to have them photographed and printed. No easy matter with only the cumbersome photographic gear available in frontier towns. I didn't dare get it done in Chicago . . . Those papers will make me, all of us, rich. You will all benefit, financially and otherwise . . . Now, that is all you need to know. The Major will go with you, Flint.'

That didn't please the sheriff: damned if he wanted that cold-eyed killer riding with him, but . . .

'Glad to have you along, Major,' he forced himself to say.

'We'll see about that. How many men you want? I'll make sure they come.'

Maybe having him along might be an advantage after all . . .

'Six or eight ought to be enough.'

'I'll pick 'em.'

'Better leave that to me. I know these men better than you.'

'I'll pick 'em,' The Major said, starting for the door. 'And I guarantee they'll come — or die where they stand . . . c'mon.'

★ ★ ★

The Major only had to shoot one man and there was no further problem in making up the numbers for the posse.

The shot man had scowled when picked to join Flint's new posse. 'I was with you before. I twisted my ankle. Can't ride again, Corey — find someone else.'

The last word was drowned by the gun shot and the man screamed and collapsed on the saloon floor, clutching his shattered foot, blood spurting across the torn boot, a white ragged edge of bone showing.

'*Now* you can't ride,' the Major said, casually swinging the smoking gun around the men already backing off. 'Need six volunteers. Don't all rush at once, fellers. I want good horsemen, riders who aren't afraid to trade a little lead with outlaws or, God forbid, even renegade Indians. Now — who wants to ride with me and Flint?'

Not five minutes later, Flint, The Major and six reluctant and fearful townsmen made their way to the livery in the late light of afternoon.

★　★　★

The rock lizard walked right across Hambone's face, bringing him out of his heat-induced torpor as if someone had lit a fire under him.

His rifle clattered amongst the rocks of the lookout area, and his heart hammered as if it would crash through his ribs. Recovering, fright driving him, he spotted the lizard scuttering away and made two savage stomps in an attempt to squash it. The reptile was way too fast, used to dodging the strike of rattlers or the lunge of coyotes. It made cover safely.

Still shaky, sweating, his breathing slowly settling, Hambone scrubbed a hand across his face, yawned and stooped to pick up his rifle. It had skidded over a small ridge and dropped a couple of feet to a flat rock below. Leaning on a handy piece of granite,

Hambone reached down and grabbed the Winchester, glad Jericho hadn't come up to check on him and caught him asleep.

He glanced up at the low-angled sun and saw it was about time to go and report in anyway. Turning away, adjusting his hat, he stopped. There was movement below! Someone down where the timber began to thin, a flash in shadow.

His heart was thudding again as he crouched, tongue licking dry lips. Damn! Riders! Two of them, and —

'Judas priest!' he breathed as he recognized Hardin and the old Indian he had seen in town lounging on the boardwalk. 'How in hell did they find our trail up here . . . ?'

But even Hambone realized the futility of speculation at this point and he dropped to one knee, levering a shell into the rifle's breech. Should he try to pick them off, letting the gunfire alert Jericho and the others, or should he go down and warn Jericho in person?

Those two below would be right up here by the time he got down to the camp and they would have the high ground then. Only one thing for it: shoot 'em down right now.

He figured Hardin would be the most dangerous, so beaded him first, following the man as he wended his way between the trees, coming now to an open space.

Hambone's finger caressed the trigger, easing it back past the first tension, intending to hold it just nudging the release point, so that as soon as he fixed his sights on Hardin it would require only minimum pressure.

But he was too shaken, excited, and took the trigger too far back: it let off as soon as he rubbed his finger up the curved metal to ease it just before he fired. He had no say in the matter then: the Winchester whipcracked and jumped in his grip, throwing the shot high. He had been aiming at Hardin's broad chest, figuring shooting downhill would be easier if he went for a body shot. Now the lead clipped Hardin's right shoulder, turning the man sharply in leather before he tumbled completely out of the saddle.

At the same time as he cursed himself for the mistake, Hambone found out that maybe the old Indian should have been his first target after all.

Hee-cha had disappeared — How? In open space between the trees like that! — and now Hardin was rolling on to his side, bringing his rifle around. He fired under the cloud of gunsmoke above Hambone's position and the young outlaw cried out in alarm as rock dust stung his eyes and sent him rearing back, the whine of the ricochet in his ears.

He clawed at his face, fumbling to lever in a fresh shell. Another bullet screamed off the rock in front of him — and then he felt a hand in his hair, pulling his head back, and the cold steel of a knife cutting the flesh of his throat. He gurgled and almost wet himself in fright as a gnarled, smelly hand closed around his jaw and squeezed his mouth shut. He began to writhe, grunting inarticulately.

'Don't kill him, Owl!' Hardin yelled from down the slope. 'We need him for a couple of minutes.'

Hambone felt the pressure of the blade ease against his neck. A little warm blood crawled over his flesh. Then he was thrown down face first and a moccasined foot slammed against the back of his neck, holding him there. Goddamn! That's the last time he makes that mistake! From now on it's shoot the Injun first, whether he's a wrinkled old walnut or a newborn babe! Even a damn squaw! Can't trust none of 'em!

Hardin's right shirtsleeve was all bloody, and red dripped from his fingers. He awkwardly tried to wad a kerchief over the wound and motioned to Owl to let Hambone sit up. The young outlaw did, spitting dirt.

'Where's Jericho, Ham? Now don't

try to stall me or Owl can easily draw that blade across your jugular.'

Hambone was afraid to be this close to dying but he wasn't short on guts. 'You don't need me to tell you where Ward is. Just wait a minute and he'll be here — with the others!'

Hardin nodded. 'Figured they wouldn't be far off.' Owl grunted and gestured down the slope on the far side of the rock-surrounded lookout. The drifter saw three men, afoot and with guns, charging up the slope from a campsite. He recognized Jericho right away.

Just as he swung up his rifle, Owl grunted again and pointed down the slope they had been climbing when Hambone had opened up.

There was a posse riding hard towards them, Flint leading. All had guns in their hands.

5

Allies?

The posse picked a way between the trees, some horses stumbling on the rough, rock-studded slope — which was why Hardin and Owl came to the lookout on foot.

While they were studying the posse, Ham came to life, kicked the old Indian's legs from under him so that he stumbled against Hardin. They tangled and Ham threw himself over the downward side, skidding and sliding, waving and yelling as dust rose around him.

'Don't shoot, Jer! Don't shoot! It's me, Hambone!'

'I oughta damn well shoot you!' Jericho shouted. 'How'd they jump you? Sleepin' as usual . . . ?'

Ham rolled, gravel-scarred, clothes torn and dusty, and came to rest only yards from the outlaws. 'No, Jer, I wasn't — I — '

Then Hardin's voice came drifting down as muted gunfire sounded on the far slope. 'Jericho! Flint's riding in with a posse and they're loaded for bear! Time we joined forces, eh?'

'You brung 'em here, you fight 'em!'

'I didn't bring 'em!'

'They trailed you!'

'They weren't even close last time Owl and me looked. It was Ham shooting at us that gave the game away.'

Jericho rounded on the hard-breathing young outlaw and Ham winced, just dodging the swing of Jericho's rifle barrel. 'I had to stop 'em, Jer! I had to!'

'C'mon, Jericho!' called Hardin. 'No time to palaver, man!'

Jericho glanced briefly at Utah and Kirk, the latter nodding curtly. 'We can use Hardin's gun.'

Jericho made his decision, yelled to Hardin to come on down. The words were hardly out of his mouth when there was a fresh burst of gunfire and then two figures dropped over the ledge and rolled and slid down towards the outlaws.

'Who's that with him? Not that smelly old Injun from town . . . ?'

'Must be,' Utah said. 'Heard him called 'Owl' once.'

Jericho's lips thinned and then the drifter and the Indian came skidding to a stop.

'Spread out!' Jericho said, sweeping an arm across the slope. 'If they're mounted we can bring down their broncs.' He glared at Hardin. 'You an' me'll talk after.'

'If we can,' Hardin answered, moving behind a tree. Owl was already by some rocks, crouching, an old cap-and-ball Navy Colt in one gnarled hand.

The Indian held up his free hand, showing four fingers, closed and opened them again. 'This many.'

'If they're all townsmen, eight won't be hard to handle,' Jericho said.

'Looked like townsmen — mostly.' The pause made all the outlaws look sharply at Hardin. 'One man wearing a cavalry hat, though, rides like the horse is part of him, and he has a rifle with a bright barrel.'

'Judas priest!'

All eyes turned to Utah McCann at his exclamation.

'Calls himself The Major! Damn killer, gun-for-hire, straight-out murderer. Uses a hand-built Henry with a thirty-inch barrel. People say he can pick the eye outta an eagle on the wing.'

'How the hell you know?' Jericho sounded sceptical.

Utah nodded, emphasizing something to himself. 'I ran into the son of a bitch in a range war up on the Wind River, year or so ago.'

'How'd you 'run into him'?' The impatience was plainly evident in Jericho's voice, one eye on the ridge and the approaching posse.

'I was ridin' for Blackjack Kidman and the other side hired this Major

. . . I tell you, we didn't last long. That son of a bitch got amongst us and picked us off one by one, sometimes two, three at a time. I said the hell with it and rode out.'

There was no more time for talk: the posse swept over the crest, having trouble with their mounts which were snorting and protesting after being whipped and spur-raked up the far slope. Their guns blazed but in wild shots, no doubt hoping to scatter the outlaws.

The bullets didn't do any harm but the stones, loosened by the sliding, whickering mounts fighting for a foothold, did the job. The driving, searching hoofs dislodged head-sized rocks and a scattering of stones causing a small avalanche.

It gathered momentum and ploughed up a wall of dirt and dust, forcing the outlaws and Hardin and the old Indian to break cover and drop further down the slope. They leapt and skidded, snatching at saplings for support, trying to slow and get under cover.

But the posse men weren't having it all their own way: their mounts were giving them real trouble and two riders had already been unseated. One of the horses fell and whinnied and kicked and slashed air wildly as it rolled and slid down-slope, forcing the outlaws to jump clear. Old Hee-cha couldn't keep up the pace and he fell. Hardin saw him go down out of the corner of his eye, managed to grab a branch and slow his own slide, threw himself across the slope using the momentum of the whippy branch like a slingshot. The Indian was grasping his ribs — likely the old bones had cracked or snapped against a rock — face contorted in pain.

Hardin scrabbled towards him, bent double, and was reaching to help him when there was a distinctive bellowing sound and suddenly Owl's head disintegrated, splashing Hardin's reaching arm with gore. He recoiled and stumbled, glancing up, saw The Major sitting his mount on a flat rock, levering a fresh shell into the long-barrelled Henry. The man, with arrogant smugness, actually grinned at Hardin as he threw the rifle to his shoulder, coldly sighting down the long, bright barrel.

Hardin spun down slope, launching himself into the air, knowing he was going to hit hard. Even as he thudded to the ground in a cloud of dust, and gravel tore at his body, the pain in his wounded shoulder drawing an involuntary grunt from him, he heard the second blast of the hand-built Henry. A strange thought exploded in his brain: If I heard the shot, it must have missed! That's if it's true you never hear the shot that kills you . . . and that's no standard rimfire cartridge, he's using. Must be hand-loads.

By then he was rolling and skidding behind a nest of rocks. One of them cracked like an egg as a third bullet from the Henry struck and snarled away, shattering into lead slivers. Damn big calibre!

He was surprised to find he still held

his rifle and squirmed in behind the rocks, laid the Winchester's barrel in a V and took a quick sight on The Major. He fired and his lead blew the cavalry hat from the killer's head. Hardin glimpsed the shock and then the murderous anger on the man's face a moment before the killer slid out of saddle and dived after the hat, staying low.

Must mean something to him, Hardin thought, turning his rifle on to the other posse men who had now dismounted and were hunting cover.

Jericho and the others were slowly backing down the slope into their campsite and the drifter guessed they would have more ammunition there. But it still wasn't a good position, not with the posse on the high ground and mounts to hand.

Then Jericho suddenly swung his rifle towards Hardin and fired. The bullet thudded into the gravel beside the drifter who instinctively rolled deeper into the rocks.

'You son of a bitch! Because of you we're gonna have to quit a damn good hideout! But you can stay! Dead or alive!'

The other outlaws started to turn their guns towards him and Hardin leapt up and ran to a small ledge and hurled himself over. Bullets whined and spurted dust and he almost passed out with the shock of pain as he landed on his right side. But he kicked against a deadfall, sending his body tumbling down the slope in a cloud of dust.

By then Jericho and the others had to give all their attention to the posse who were working their way down, raking the slopes. He heard the Henry's deep-throated bark several times.

Then he rolled onto a grassy bench, slid easily over the long stalks and dropped over the edge. He found himself in a neat little boulder-ringed hollow where Jericho and his men had tethered their horses on long grazing ropes — already saddled. Careful man, Jericho . . .

The palomino was closest, raised its head and stared at him with large, clear, amber eyes even as it chewed on sweetgrass.

Despite his pain and his aching body, Hardin brushed what dirt he could from his rifle and then limped towards the horse. His wound was bleeding quite badly now, his grimy shirtsleeve sodden with his blood. But he switched the rifle to that hand, sticky though it was, kept his left side towards the horse in case the close smell of blood made it nervous. Tentatively, he reached out with his left hand.

'Well, boy, looks like you and me're finally gonna get acquainted.'

There was nothing he could do for old Owl and nothing he wanted to do for Jericho and his pards. No point in sticking around . . .

He stroked the palomino's neck, talking quiet, meaningless words, the tone of his voice soothing to the animal, but it was still mighty leery, eyes wide. Never a good sign. Wide eyes in a horse mean trouble's not far off. He looked at the ears: OK so far, kind of horizontal: the animal was still curious, but ready if its instincts warned of impending trouble. He managed to grab the bridle and stepped close, raising the horse's head and letting its quivering nostrils come to rest a bare inch from his face. He smelled the hot breath but knew the palomino was smelling him, too, taking in the pheromones he was releasing, decoding them into how Hardin really felt about him.

Hardin had thought such things were fanciful when first demonstrated by a man named Bronco Madigan — who turned out to be an undercover US Marshal — but he sure knew horses, that Madigan. Some said he was part horse himself.

And now once again the truth of Madigan's methods became apparent. The palomino's ears lifted to their upright position, the head shook and the eyes settled into normal viewing position. The big jaw nudged his arm and Hardin gave it an extra pat: the palomino was willing to trust him. And all this had taken only seconds.

Now, from up the slope, the gunfire intensified and he figured the sooner he got clear of the area the better.

As he mounted and dropped out of sight down the far side of the bench, the shooting behind him sounded like the Battle of the Little Bighorn.

'Shoot their goddamn mounts!' yelled Jericho, face grimy with powdersmoke and sweat and dirt.

The posse had split: half keeping up a withering fire so as to pin down the outlaws, the others getting the mounts. It was clear Flint was going to risk a charge down the dangerously steep slope. Plumb loco to even contemplate!

Normally, Jericho would let the lawmen find out for themselves just how risky it was, trying to ride fast with such broken ground dropping steeply under the hoofs of nervous mounts that were far from being sure-footed in such terrain. Let 'em spill and break bones!

is what he would normally say.

But there were still eight of them, although he thought two had been wounded, though not badly enough to put them out of the fight. Even if only half of them were still able to shoot after taking a tumble, those were odds that Jericho didn't care for, not with amunition running so low.

'Shoot the hosses before they mount!' he bawled again and all four outlaws turned their fire on the group who had now reached the mounts.

But they hadn't allowed for the odd man out: The Major. He was sitting snugly amongst some rocks, the big Henry's burnished octagonal barrel resting in a natural groove. He worked the lever three times, deliberate actions, but fast and sure. There were three miniature eruptions of earth down the slope and Kirk was lifted off his feet, driven backwards a couple of yards by the heavy bullet that took him in the right upper thigh. He slammed to earth in a writhing heap, moaning, grasping at the bloody wound.

Jericho and the others stayed down but Kirk, though hurting, still held his rifle and while The Major tried to get a clear shot at the others, he brought it up, gritted his teeth with the effort of holding it steady and squeezed off his shot. It struck the rock in front of The Major's face and the man reared back, dropping his precious rifle, clawing at his stinging cheeks and eyes.

It was good enough for Jericho: he and Utah and Hambone rose from cover and hammered a barrage into the possemen still trying to control the skittish, prancing, snorting mounts. The men dropped behind cover and two horses reared, whinnying and pawing the air before crashing over on their sides, kicking. The posse men who had been left to rake the outlaws spun around carelessly, to see if one of the downed animals might be theirs.

Two went down under the heavy fire from the outlaws and the rest scattered, unwilling to risk their necks on this dangerous mountain slope. Flint was yelling something but had to duck as lead burned across one cheek, slashed the lobe of the ear on that side.

There was a lot of yelling up there and Jericho saw The Major had a kerchief up to his face and it was blood-spotted. He put the last two bullets in his magazine into the rocks, saw the killer drop hurriedly. Jericho bared his teeth. 'Time to go, gents!'

'What about Kirk?' gasped Hambone.

Jericho was about to say 'Leave him!' but something told him Kirk might still be needed: he had not yet studied and fully interpreted those papers from the sealed valise. Jericho had a hunch they might just lead to a lot of money.

'You and Utah carry him,' he said, thumbing fresh loads into the rifle's under-barrel magazine tube. 'I'll cover you.'

It wasn't an easy retreat. Flint mobilized three possemen and they potshotted at the fleeing outlaws, concentrating on the men carrying the wounded Kirk. But their hearts weren't in it and the outlaws knew every inch of this slope and the mountains. They made it to the cave and when they looked back up the slope, they were in time to see the last of the posse retreating over the crest, the remaining mounts running free. Two wounded men lay calling and cursing on this side of the mountain.

'That'll keep 'em busy, tryin' to catch the broncs that're left,' Utah panted with satisfaction.

They bandaged Kirk's wound roughly, gathered what gear they needed and slipped out of the cave by a low, hidden tunnel that took them to within ten yards of the grazing area for their mounts. Jericho skidded to a halt instantly.

'My palomino's gone!' He swore. 'That goddamn Hardin! C'mon! He don't know this country — we can catch him easy!'

'Hell Jer! Flint'll be on our tails again soon as he finds the pass through the range!' Utah sounded really worried.

'He'll do it, too,' Kirk gritted, wound roughly bandaged, supported by both Utah and Hambone. 'Stubborn as a Missouri mule!'

'We can't palaver now!' Utah said, nerves sounding in his voice. 'We gotta move before they regroup!'

Jericho raked both with hard eyes. 'Well, let's save our butts first. But don't think I'm lettin' Hardin get off with my hoss! I'll find the son of a bitch. I'll find him — you can bet his life on that!'

6

No Rest

But it wasn't going to be as easy as that.

Kirk had said it all when he had told Jericho that Flint was as stubborn as a Missouri mule.

The sheriff raged at the posse's survivors, although he was careful not to include The Major in any of his harangues. The wounded men were tended to on the spot, only one, named King, seriously hurt. Flint would not agree to one of the unhurt men escorting the wounded back to town.

'We got three walking-wounded, and one of them can ride OK so he'll come with us. The other two are fit enough to get King back for the sawbones to look at. The rest of us'll find a way through these damn mountains even if we have to go all the way up to Manitou Pass.'

'Ain't gonna be easy,' one man allowed, 'Findin' the pass or Jericho — we's none of us real trackers worth a hill of beans. Course, if we still had old Owl . . . '

He flicked his eyes briefly in the direction of The Major then glanced away quickly, let his words end abruptly.

'I'll see the wounded back to town,' The Major told Flint, startling the sheriff.

'Well, I was kinda countin' on you comin' along, Major. You and that portable cannon.'

'Mr Macauley'll want me with him, or if he don't he'll be the one to gimme my orders.'

That put Flint in his place and the sheriff obviously didn't like it. But he sighed, accepting.

'OK, the rest of us'll try to pick up the trail of them outlaws. Can you send us some more men, Major? They might listen to you . . . '

The Major's thin lips twitched, the closest he came to smiling. 'They'll join you if I say so.' Flat. No argument.

It made Flint feel a little easier. 'We'll leave a few blaze marks for you,' he said as the posse broke up and went their separate ways. The sheriff knew he had a bunch of mutinous riders with him but they, too, had seen The Major in action by now and he didn't anticipate any real problems.

It might be a tough job finding a way through the ranges, but Flint would do it somehow: he would find the trail he wanted, and sooner or later catch up with Jericho and his outlaws. He didn't mind being out here, actually, away from Macauley's wrath. Let Borden take the brunt of it. This time the damn banker had played it too close to his chest, not telling him Mac's valise and private papers were in the safe. Well, now he could explain to Macauley . . . Maybe!

Cole Hardin's part in all this still remained a question mark as far as

Corey Flint was concerned: seemed to him there was some kind of connection between the drifter and the outlaws. But he would catch up with him, too, sooner or later. You could bet your britches on that.

★　★　★

The palomino knew more about the country than Hardin.

Just as well, too, for the wound was giving him hell and though he wadded kerchiefs and tore up his shirt — using a fresh one from Jericho's saddle-bags to wear — he was still losing blood. That fall had busted the wound wide open, and it was mighty hard to staunch the flow of blood.

He felt light-headed and awkwardly roped himself to the saddle, a couple of turns around his thighs, tying off on the saddle-horn. He held on with his right hand although there was not full strength in his grip now. He carried the Winchester across his thighs, using his bloody forearm to put enough pressure on the weapon to keep it from falling.

The palomino seemed to know where it was going so he let it have its head. From what he had picked up in the card game and Flint had told him, Silk had been a man with a lot of different interests, not all of them above board. He went after what he wanted and didn't much care how he obtained it. Without going into details, Flint had hinted that that included the palomino. Hardin had the notion that it had belonged to someone who had a ranch in the foothills. Which could explain how come the horse travelled this country so confidently.

Hardin knew the danger he was in. He couldn't stop and dismount and try to cover his tracks. He was leaving spots of blood, too, but the way he was feeling right now, he didn't much care if Jericho or Flint or even that damn murdering 'Major' caught up with him. He was almost at the point of past caring what happened.

The horse plodded on and Hardin swayed in the saddle, head throbbing, body racked with pain. Then he jerked his head up in alarm and said aloud, words slurred, 'Hell! Be sundown right soon.'

The palomino grunted as if it knew the dangers of oncoming night and it seemed to Hardin that it increased its pace. But he slouched in the saddle, head filling with wild, phantom thoughts and images as the horse came down out of the deepening shadows of the ranges on to rolling grassland.

The last thing he remembered for some time was seeing a flash in the distance up ahead on a small hogback rise.

Like the westering sun reflecting from glass.

★　★　★

Kirk had been with Jericho for a long time now and while normally he would have abandoned a wounded man if he figured he would slow him down, Jericho still had use for Kirk. Those papers from the sealed valise still had to be studied properly.

So, just before sundown, he called a halt in a draw that was timbered on three sides and agreed to light a small fire and boil some water for treating Kirk's wound. There was a ragged piece of flesh gouged out by the large projectile from The Major's special gun. The wound was dirty from where Kirk had fallen and he kept asking if he was going to lose his leg: it seemed to be a genuine fear.

'How the hell do I know?' snapped Jericho, a frustrated and angry man after the day's happenings. 'We'll clean and flush it out with hot water and bandage it before you bleed to death. That's about as far as we can take it, Kirk.'

'Drop me close to town, so I can get to a sawbones,' Kirk asked. It was the first time any of them had seen fear in the man, heard it in his voice. And, unlike him, he didn't seem to want to stop talking, prattled on all the time, driven by nerves and anxiety, Jericho suspected.

He seemed eager for them to know why he was here, an almost-qualified lawyer, riding the owlhoot trail . . .

He told them for the first time how, years ago, when assisting a senior lawyer defending a man charged with a horrendous crime against a woman and her two children, he had found a loophole in the law that favoured the accused. His senior had pounced upon it, for it looked certain the prisoner would hang otherwise and here was a possible way out. The senior was a man who had never, *never*, lost a case. With a powerful and histrionic speech, with many gestures and pauses for effect, he brought the loophole to the judge's attention and asked for a ruling. After a sleepless overnight consideration the judge decided that, although he felt, personally, the accused was guilty, according to the law, he shouldn't be on trial. The undetailed loophole discovered by Kirk allowed the case to be dismissed and the killer to go free.

'They got him, though,' Kirk said, grim-faced, head nodding at the memory. 'They got him in the end. During the time he was free, he committed the same sort of atrocity on another family. *That* was the one they got him for and he was eventually hanged. But it was too late! *Too late*, dammit! Because of me, my eagerness to show I could be a damned good lawyer, that second family suffered the terrors of hell. Those poor kids — ' He paused, eyes filling as the memories shook him. 'I — I had a child of my own. I couldn't stand it. I decided if the law was so foolish it offered monsters like that an extra chance to commit more crimes, I wanted no part of it. So I quit . . . left my family. Rode West.'

'Yeah, yeah, OK,' Jericho said tiredly. 'We savvy how come you ride the owlhoot. Now you rest up. We'll take care of you. Study them papers we got from the bank safe. It'll help take your mind off your pain . . . '

Under his breath he added, 'Either that or I take a gun butt to you to blame well shut you up!'

But not long after, Jericho was mighty glad the wounded Kirk was able to read, and interpret, those papers.

The outlaws were sitting around the small campfire, smoking a last cigarette before turning in, when Kirk's voice startled them all.

'Ward! Ward! My God, d'you know what I've got here?'

'Now how the hell would I know that?' growled Jericho turning his head, making no effort to stand.

Kirk was lying under a slight overhang that reflected light from the fire and his face was all shadows and hollows, etched with pain. But there was a brightness in his eyes that wasn't caused by rising fever. He held up the handful of papers.

'These are railroad papers! The Michigan and Western Line — They're

Union Pacific's rivals — There're some schedules and freight lists we might be able to use, but mostly these are the special reports on future expansion, circulated amongst the company heads! With recommendations for shareholders and . . . '

'Christ, you think I'm interested in that!'

Jericho heaved to his feet and went across to squat down by Kirk. He reached for the papers but Kirk, ignoring the gesture, held them in front of him, lifting two or three pages before turning the others to face Jericho.

'See? Here — a report on proposed land acquisition — rights-of-way through cattle country and farmland — a surveyor's recommendations for what land to purchase, other areas marked as possibilities — pending geological tests for ground stability . . . '

Jericho scowled, dropped his hand now. 'Jesus Christ! That kinda borin' stuff's no good to us I tell you! Nothin' in there about payroll trains, is there . . . ?'

'There could be — I haven't gone right through yet. But, Ward, if someone knew what land the railroad was planning to buy up and moved in before word got out, he could double, even treble, his money!'

'The hell're you talkin' about?' Jericho impatiently snatched the pages from Kirk, one tearing. He scanned them cursorily, flipping them over one by one. 'I *ain't* interested in this kinda hogwash, Kirk . . . whoa! Wait! What's this? List of payroll shipments to the silver mine at Spanish Bluff! Now that's more like it. An' here's when the mine plant figures to ship silver bullion down to Denver! Only tentative dates but close enough for us to work by.' He turned to Kirk as the others came across now. 'Boys, with these, we're gonna be mighty rich! We take it easy till one of these dates comes round, then go hit the train and help ourselves.'

Hambone started crowing like a rooster until Utah elbowed him in the ribs. But his tongue ran over his dry lips and his eyes were bright. 'You reckon it'll work, Jer?'

'Well, we mighta done some fool things from time to time, but I can't see where we can go wrong here — eh, Kirk?'

Kirk was suffering a bout of great pain right then, gasping, face twisted, hand holding his wounded leg. 'In my — experience, nothing's that — easy! You gotta plan — carefully.'

'Aah, what're you talkin' about?' growled Jericho. 'This is easy, an' don't worry none, Kirk. You'll get your share even if you can't ride along with us. You've already earned your money.'

Kirk sank back, the night world spinning about him.

Just before he passed out, he thought, the fools have already forgotten there's a posse out hunting them down. And do they think those express cars won't be heavily guarded? He closed his eyes and hoped he would fall asleep quickly. And wouldn't dream about trying to go through the rest of his life with only one leg.

★   ★   ★

Marcus Macauley was a perfect gentleman and succeeded in charming Banker Borden's wife and their two young daughters, one ten, the other almost twelve and showing the first small buds of developing womanhood.

His manners were excellent and he entertained them with anecdotes from Chicago, dazzled them with descriptions of the Windy City and the progress of burgeoning technology.

After the meal and the little girls were sent to bed, the men smoked cigars over brandy in Borden's small den while Mrs Borden supervised the servants in clearing away the supper things.

'Wonderful family, Harrison,' Macauley said, waving his thick cigar and swirling the brandy in the cut crystal glass. 'I envy you.'

Borden was pleased, beginning to relax now, the knot of nervousness bordering on pure terror in his belly at last starting to unravel.

'Why, thank you, Mac, it's been a pleasure having you. You should visit more often.'

He knew at once it was the wrong thing to say. It gave Macauley the opening he wanted. 'Not under anything like the present circumstances, Harrison, I assure you.'

Borden felt the knot tighten again and suddenly the rich cigar smoke felt harsh and searing, the brandy tasted sour on his palate — the glass rim even rattled briefly against his teeth. Macauley's bleak eyes rested steadily on his blanched features.

'An unforgivable mistake, Harrison.'

'But that damn Jericho broke into the safe! He must've had a blasted *key*! I was given to understand that the one I had was the only emergency key in existence. The blame can be placed way back up the line from me, Mac.

114

Someone duplicated that key. It has to be that way.'

Macauley's gaze didn't warm any but after a few unsettling moments he nodded slightly. 'Perhaps I am being a little too harsh, but this is one of the most important sets of papers I've ever been able to get my hands on! And it cost me plenty to do it. I'm taking one hell of a risk but I'll never have such a chance as this again.' He stood abruptly and moved jerkily around the small room, banged against a chair arm and spilled some brandy.

'Dammit, Harrison! I wish you had a decent-size den! There's no room to swing a cat in here!'

'It's quite large, actually, for the type of houses we build out here, Mac.'

Macauley scowled, dismissed it with a wave of his cigar again. 'Harrison, I will tell you something. I have many financial commitments as you know from our past . . . association. They call me a 'speculator' and that's a very good description. But to be successful at it I have to grab the chances when they come, and this can tie up a man's funds, while waiting for them to bring in the expected profits.'

Despite his complaint about the room being small, Macauley began to pace around the perimeter, frowning, head bowed, hands now clasped behind his back. He paused opposite Borden's chair, looking down at him very gravely.

'Those papers name specific areas the Michigan and Western Railroad Company intends to buy so as to extend their system in this area, pushing west through Southern Utah and across the Nevada narrow-neck, ultimately, all the way to San Francisco.'

Borden couldn't help but be impressed by this news. 'My God! With the link they already have from the east they — they'll span the continent!'

'Yes, other railroads already have the same thing in mind, Union Pacific in particular, and they would love to get their hands on those papers. It's possible, when I get the papers back, that I will be able to make a very profitable deal with one of the companies, but also, with the knowledge of where Michigan and Western are planning to run their rights-of-way, I, and some selected friends, could invest in that very land . . . '

He paused, watching Borden closely. The banker smiled slowly. 'And more or less ask your own price?'

'Not just ask it, Harrison, but we would get it! M and W are committed! They would have to pay whatever we ask.'

Borden gulped some brandy. His hand was shaking a little: he might be nervous, but there was nothing wrong with the way his brain was functioning where finances and smart deals such as Macauley offered were concerned.

'And you want my bank to finance the purchase of this land, Mac?'

Macauley raked up one of his charming smiles. 'Of course, Harrison! I've already explained that my — er

— financial hands are hogtied right now. Wildwood is ideally situated. The land in question is within the boundaries of or bordering Sawatch County — a good deal of it, anyway, some very close to the pass through the sierras.'

'Manitou Pass? Why, of course! It's the easiest way through the sierra chain.'

'Yes. No tunnelling required . . . can you imagine what kind of a price a railroad would pay for right-of-way to the land either end of that pass, Harrison?' He smiled crookedly. 'You will no doubt understand now why I am travelling under the protection of The Major.'

Borden blew out his cheeks, reached for the brandy decanter. 'I think this calls for some kind of toast, Mac!'

Macauley held out his glass and when both were full, he lifted his to face-level, and, bleak gaze on the banker's face, said soberly, 'To the recovery of the papers, without which the best laid plans of mice and men will amount to *nothing*!'

Borden drank, but the fine brandy was tasteless in his dry mouth.

He knew he ought to be feeling elated — that's if he read Macauley right: he would be cut in for a share.

But through his nervousness and the brandy's fumes, he knew only too well that he was being used. And could therefore be discarded by a man like Macauley whenever it suited him.

With the aid of the awesome Major.

Harrison Borden began to wonder if any amount of riches would be worth that risk.

7

We Hang Horse Thieves

He didn't know if it was the crack of the rifle or the whine of the bullet that woke him from his doze in the saddle.

The palomino jerked up its head and swerved to one side and Hardin swayed wildly, tightening his grip on the horn. His hand was sticky with half-congealed blood but he managed to stay in leather, looking around him in the dim light. Dusk, he thought.

'Lift your hands and hold that bronc right where it is, mister!'

The hard voice came down to him from some boulders piled against the bottom of a small cliff, remnants of an old rockfall. Hardin heard the lever of a rifle clash as it jacked another cartridge into the breech.

'Get them hands up, dammit!'

'Can only move one arm,' Hardin said, strain in his voice. 'I've been shot.'

'And damn close to bein' shot again! Do like I say!'

Hardin lifted his left arm out from his side. He could do little with the wounded right and apparently the rifleman saw this. 'All right. Just stay put while I come down.'

He was a bow-legged cowpoke, in his forties, Hardin guessed. Not exactly mean-looking, but tough and no-nonsense. He walked around to the front of the palomino, rifle angled up at Hardin all the time. He squinted a little. 'We hang hoss thieves in this country, feller!'

'I've heard that.'

'Then what you doin' on that palomino?'

'It's mine.'

'Like hell! Belongs to a man named Hi-spade Silk — not that he come by it dead-honest, I allow — Hoss's name is 'Ace' on account Silk is a gambler.'

'Was — he lost a hand to me. This was part of the pot.' Hardin patted the neck of the palomino with his blood-caked right hand.

'He'd never put up Ace in a card game!'

'He done it.'

The cowboy frowned, aware of Hardin's feverish though steady stare. 'Got a name?' Hardin told him. 'Never heard of you. Drifter?' Cole nodded wearily. 'Silk shoot you?'

'No. Feller named Hambone.'

'What kinda name is that?'

'Nickname. He's called that but his real monicker is 'Hambleton'. If it makes any difference.'

'How come he shot you?'

'Judas, you ask a lot of questions.'

'An' I want answers.' The cowboy jerked his rifle to draw Hardin's attention to it, as if he might have forgotten it was covering him.

Taking a deep breath, Hardin gave him an abbreviated version of events. The cowboy was silent after Hardin finished speaking, sagging now in the saddle. 'Well, it's a good story, I guess. You sure look tuckered. I better take you in.'

Hardin stiffened. 'Where?'

The other chuckled. 'Not back to Flint, so don't worry. The Carnavan spread is a coupla miles around that butte. We'll make up our mind about you when we get there.'

Hardin nodded and the cowboy whistled through his teeth, twice, startling him. A shaggy cowpony came trotting around the rockpile and the rifleman mounted easily, the gun not wavering hardly at all from Hardin's direction. The barrel jerked warningly.

'Ride on ahead, I'll call directions.'

★　★　★

It took till full dark to reach the spread and Hardin figured this might have been the place where the sun struck against a window earlier. It would be in about the right position.

There was a dull light showing in a small bunkhouse and a man filled the doorway, a cup of coffee in one hand, the other resting on his holstered Colt.

'What you got there, Spud?'

'Feller been shot, forkin' Silk's palomino.'

'Sounds interestin'. Glory's up to the house. I'll tag along.'

'They shoulda called you 'Sticky' 'stead of 'Stock''

'Stock's my name and I'm proud of it.' He looked younger than Spud but only by a few years. He reached up to a peg, jammed a hat on his head and, still sipping from the cup, followed the riders up to the house.

Hardin was told to dismount and he fumbled at the rope holding him in place, then tumbled out of leather and crashed to the ground, letting out an involuntary cry of pain.

Everything was shot through with whirling bright lights until it all suddenly went black.

★ ★ ★

Then there was bright sunshine and he saw he was in a room with a woman whose hair took on a deep amber fire as she walked past the window. She paused, looking down at him in the narrow bed.

'So, you've decided to join us.' Her voice was level and easy to listen to. Hardin blinked, his eyes gritty, but not so gritty he didn't notice she was medium tall, and was wearing a blue-and-white check calico dress which she filled pleasingly.

'I'm Gloria Carnavan. You're in my spare room. I've cleaned and dressed your wound and I think most of the infection is going now.'

He frowned, thinking about her words. 'Infection — takes time to — clear, don't it?'

She smiled, teeth white against her tanned face. 'Today's your third here. Silk's palomino gave us some concern but Spud went to town and learned what had happened.'

'I already told him.'

'We had to check. You told the truth.'

'Easiest way — er — Flint still looking for me?'

'I believe so, but I think you no longer have priority. Seems he's after a man named Jericho. Something to do with a bank robbery and now a train derailment.'

That startled Hardin. 'When was this . . . ? I know about the bank robbery, but derailing *a train* . . . ?'

'I don't know any details. Only that Flint had been wandering the hills trying to find you when he got urgent word about the train wreck. It was deliberate, by all counts.'

Hardin held his silence. Jericho must have gone off the rails to start derailing trains. Then he realized what he had said to himself and couldn't help but smile a little.

'Something amusing?' the girl asked.

'No, not amusing at all, just some fool thought I had . . . I'm obliged for your help, Miss Carnavan. I'll gladly pay for any trouble I've given you . . . '

'We'll talk about that later perhaps. You just lie abed for another day or so.'

'I can't do that! I've imposed too much already.'

She studied his drawn features for a few moments, then smiled slowly. 'When *I* think you're imposing on me, I'll let you know.'

He nodded, weariness overtaking him so that he realized he was a lot weaker than he figured. There were some things to be straightened out, too: Where was the palomino? Why hadn't she turned him in to Sheriff Flint anyway? How come Spud was so concerned about Silk?

There were too many things for his tired brain to handle and despite himself, he drifted off into another sleep.

★ ★ ★

Ward Jericho and his outlaws had travelled a long way in a couple of days, south and slightly east, to where the railroad skirted Black Canyon alongside the Gunnison River.

They had studied the 'tentative' time schedules on the pages Kirk had and Jericho had placed a stubby finger with a broken, black-rimmed nail on one name: Schifflin's Bridge.

'A bridge is always a good place to stop a train,' he said.

Kirk, suffering a lot of pain from his wound, spoke in gasps. 'That's only a — possible — run — not certain. You could go — all that — way and — find it's only a — freight. This — is just a — guide — I told you that.'

'An' you done good, but we can't sit around doin' nothin'. That bank money's burnin' a hole in Ham's and Utah's pockets — not to mention yours truly's — so we go for Delta, have us a little fun, then hit that train's express car.' He beamed around at Utah and Hambone. 'Make sense?'

They were both quick to agree: the prospect of kicking up their heels while

128

they had full pockets appealed to them. Kirk shook his head.

'Don't — waste your time — Ward! It's not certain-sure. Anyway, it might be only a passenger train. You can't go by that timetable!'

'So? We miss the train or it ain't what we want, we go on back to Delta if we got any *dinero* left an' hooraw it a mite more!'

'What about — me?'

Jericho made his face sad. 'Aw, you'll be OK here for a few days. Flint'll never find this place. We've left iodine and some rags — you can reach your wound OK. Some hardtack, too, and Ham'll fill the canteens before we go.'

Kirk's eyes were bright and not just with fever. 'I don't guess you'll be leaving my share with me?'

Jericho smiled widely. 'Now what good would that do? No way you could spend it. We might's well use it. We'll owe you, square-up next time we have somethin' to split.'

Kirk didn't argue. He knew he was

being abandoned. If he made too much fuss, Jericho was likely to put a bullet in him. At least he had some small chance this way, if they left him just as he was.

★ ★ ★

They did, and none of them gave him any further thought as they raced their mounts to Black Canyon, their minds mostly recalling the delights of Delta.

Kirk had been right: the tentative schedule as laid down had not been adhered to and there was no sign of the train. So they went into Delta again and gave it a few more coats of red paint in one wild night, wasting what was left of the stolen bank money on women and booze and cards — and more of the same.

The Delta stores and saloons and cathouses were sorry to see them go, three wrung-out, head-thumping, raw-gutted revellers slinking out of town, swearing never to touch a glass of rotgut again nor even look in the direction of any sweet-smelling blousy woman.

Through their heavy hangovers they knew they had been cheated and robbed. It hadn't bothered them at the time while they still had money to keep right on funning, but now it riled them and Jericho said it was time to wait out that goddamn train. It had to come sooner or later. They knew it hadn't been through yet because Delta was awaiting delivery of badly wanted stores.

Which should have told them the train would be mostly freight.

And it was. They spotted it through Jericho's field glasses from a knoll above the plains where the rails, after picking up from a wide, swinging curve, ran like a glittering arrow, straight as a knife edge, towards the bridge over the river canyon.

'Ah, *shoot!*' Jericho snapped. 'Look at them freight cars and open wagons! No damn express cars there!'

Utah was nursing a hangover still and

131

he said, 'Hell with it, Jer, let's go hide out someplace till the next one comes. I swear my gut'll turn inside out if I throw up one more time.'

'Surely is disappointin',' Hambone said, in better shape than the others, maybe because of his youth. 'Oughta teach the damn railroad a lesson, disappointin' us like that.' He spat surly, young vacant face now showing anger.

Jericho turned his head slowly and looked at Hambone. '*Yeah!*' he said, almost smiling. 'Why the hell not?'

They had plenty of time to beat the train to the bridge which crossed the ravine with the river far below, starting just beyond the end of the cutting.

Hangovers deliberately pushed to the backs of their minds now, they climbed to the top of the cutting wall, tethering their mounts back in the trees and, using a long sun-hardened sapling, prised a heavy boulder out of its resting place. It teetered on the edge above the rail-line which was beginning to hum and tremble slightly now with the approach of the train.

The outlaws were sweating, muscles aching, wondering what craziness had made them even contemplate such a *loco* move as this. But they felt stubborn, too, and, anyway, all was ready now so somehow their frustrations and booze-fuelled anger was all directed at the railroad — represented now by the approaching nine-car freight. The locomotive whistled in an echoing shrill scream, and they clapped their hands over their ears, wincing, then cussing the engineer.

'Grab your levers, boys,' Jericho said, setting the example. 'When the loco passes under us, send 'er down! It'll smash into the first or second cars and the loco'll veer into the wall, the rest of the cars'll pile into it! She'll be a mighty fine wreck! An' make them rich bastards dig deep to repair this length of track!'

But it didn't work that way. The huge boulder had settled back some into its original hole in the cutting wall. The locomotive passed below and the boulder barely moved with their efforts. Jericho swore and made ugly threats as they strained and heaved and sweated — and finally the big rock began to move creakingly towards the edge.

'More! More!' panted Jericho and they all made one last concerted effort.

The rock toppled into space and crash-landed between the fifth and sixth boxcars, splintering both, smashing on through the couplings to mangle the rails. The loco lurched and swayed with the sudden impact and the immense jarring ran clear through the couplings all the way to the metal floor-plates of the cab, throwing the crew around roughly. The locomotive swerved mightily, jumped the shuddering, twisting rails and headed straight for the ravine, just missing the end of the bridge, dragging all five cars and the tender with it. There were metallic screeches and rumblings and clatterings as the train hurtled to its doom, cars spilling freight and a couple of screaming men.

From far below, out of the rending of metal against rock, the hiss of scalding steam as the loco rolled into shallow water, came a blossoming of fire. There was a dull explosion hard on its heels, followed by a blistering blast of hot air and debris.

Wood splintered as the cars and freight were turned into matchwood and a disgusting mess of mangled food containers and crushed men.

The booming drummed away slowly and, as silence began to settle beneath the thick, swirling smoke clouds, a rooster crowed several times.

Or a good imitation of one.

8

Storm

Flint's posse found only the guard alive, sprawling among the shattered remains of the caboose. He was bleeding from head injuries, had two ribs poking through his skin and a long, jagged splinter impaling his left leg.

He seemed to be unconscious but he screamed as the possemen cut through the large splinter so they could tie him to a horse. But he swiftly dropped back into oblivion.

They scouted around and read the sign: it was obvious a group of men had deliberately rolled a boulder down onto the train as it passed through the cutting, just a few yards this side of Schifflin's Bridge.

'Them tracks are the same ones we

followed from the bank, Sheriff,' said Reece Daimler, a one-time wolf-hunter who could read tracks almost as good as an Indian. 'Reckon there's no secret who done this — Jericho and his bunch.'

The man frowned as Flint nodded and then as Daimler started to swing away, the sheriff said, 'Why you lookin' like that?'

Daimler, a leathery-faced stringbean of a man, frowned and looked wary. 'Like what?'

'Like you ain't sure.'

'About what?'

'About them tracks, dammit! Don't play dumb-ass with me, Reece! I ain't in the mood.'

'That don't surprise me none, Corey. You can be one cantankerous s.o.b. at times.' Seeing the sheriff's face tighten, Daimler swiftly held up a hand, and said, 'OK — the tracks are Jericho's, I'll swear to that — but seems to me there's only three hosses. We started out trailin' *four*.'

'One of 'em's been hit!' Flint said, and a couple of other men nodded in agreement.

'Killed, I wouldn't wonder,' spoke up one townsman. 'We sure poured the lead into 'em. Make Mr Winchester right happy to know how many bullets we shot off.'

'Don't think he'd be dead,' opined Reece Daimler. 'They'd've kept his hoss as a spare if he was an' there's only tracks of three riders around here.'

Flint frowned, looking thoughtful, hand scratching at the grimy stubble on his lantern jaw. His bullet-burned ear had long ago stopped bleeding but there was dried blood caked on his neck and stiffening his shirt collar. He would not be sorry to get back to town to clean up, but now with the possibility that Jericho had abandoned a wounded man somewhere . . .

'We'll split up,' he decided. 'Reece, you take two men and scout around, backtrack these bastards — might even lead you to their hideout. If so, send someone to town and we'll bring us a big posse this time, pin 'em down, and either shoot 'em all or hang the survivors from the nearest tree.'

It wasn't a popular decision with either Daimler or the two men he chose, because dark rain clouds were building above the ranges. But they all reluctantly agreed Flint had come up with a good move that might pay off. If it didn't, well, they'd just be a day or so later arriving back to their homes and families.

The sawbones managed to bring the train guard out of his unconscious state not long after Flint left him at the infirmary. The doctor sent a messenger and the sheriff hurried across. The guard was in great pain and his head rolled a lot on his neck, his head heavily bandaged.

'Be quick, Sheriff,' the doctor snapped. 'I aim to give him a stiff dose of laudanum to ease his pain. Now, Shep, what is it you want to tell the sheriff?'

Shep tried to focus but kept blinking and shaking his head until he moaned aloud. Then he said, all in a rush, ''Twas Jericho, Corey — seen him on the cuttin' wall . . . '

'Did you manage to decipher that?' the medico asked and Flint had only just started to nod when he was shouldered aside and the doctor held a glass of brown liquid to the injured man's battered mouth. 'Here — drink this down, Shep. It'll ease your pain.' He looked over his shoulder at the lawman. 'I don't know how he can stand it — be lucky if that leg doesn't have to come off. But he just wouldn't give in until he'd seen you.'

Flint nodded, squeezed Shep's shoulder gently. 'Thanks *amigo*. Thanks a lot.'

Outside the infirmary Flint paused as he put his hat on, glancing up at the lowering sky. The Major was waiting for him, face as grim as ever.

'Mr Macauley wants to see you.'

'I gotta get a posse together — '

The Major didn't speak again, merely grabbed Flint by the upper arm and started walking, the lawman having to skip a little until he was in step alongside.

'Judas! Cut it out! Whole damn town's watchin'!'

'Shut up and come.'

Flint did but tugged at his arm a few times, finally saying, through gritted teeth, 'I swear, Major, you don't let go that arm, I'll shoot you!'

He dropped his hand to his gun butt and The Major looked faintly amused. 'Upset the little man's feelings, have I? OK, but you dawdle and I'll be the one doing the shooting.'

Flint refrained from rubbing his arm which was aching from the gunfighter's iron grip. It was still burning when rain started falling and they began to jog-trot down the boardwalk. The Major led the way into Macauley's hotel as a real downpour started, roaring on the roofs and turning the dusty street to mud. The sheriff was surprised to see Banker Borden in Macauley's room as it was the middle of the day.

But noticing the look on Macauley's face, Flint figured he would get in first, give himself a little credit right from the start. 'The guard's just told me it was definitely Jericho who dropped that boulder on the train.'

Macauley's eyes narrowed. 'I thought so — I also thought you'd have Jericho in jail by now, or better still, lying in a shallow grave in some remote corner of the wilderness!'

Flint, annoyed at himself for letting this cold-eyed sonuver upset him so easily, made his excuses, gave a brief version of the posse's long chase.

'I noticed there was only three tracks on top of the cuttin',' Flint said, deciding it wouldn't hurt to give himself an extra pat on the back. 'Figured it meant one of Jericho's men was wounded, maybe dead. So I sent a couple men under Reece Daimler to backtrack. Reece is mighty good — a wolf hunter. Wish he'd been available right from the start.'

'Let's hope he's as good as you say,' Macauley said and Flint glanced at the silent, worried-looking Borden.

The banker spoke up slowly. 'Mac's worried that they've read the papers from the valise. There were tentative timetables and he figures that freight train was on the list.'

Macauley caught Flint's gaze now. 'If Jericho uses those timetables to start holding up or wrecking trains, as long as he's free to do it, the railroad will soon change it's mind about trying to run a line through this country. They have alternatives, which I don't know about yet, and that means I'll lose a lot of money I've already invested — and I won't make the killing I'd hoped for around here.'

Flint nodded slowly, thinking: Mac needs the money bad! He's just showed us a chink in his armour and don't yet realize it. Thing is, how to use that knowledge . . . ?

'So, I want you to get together another posse, a dedicated one this time, Corey,' Macauley was saying. 'And I want Jericho and his gang wiped off the face of the earth!' He looked both deadly and desperate, eyes bleak, lips compressed. Then there was a flicker of puzzled doubt as he didn't see the expected flash of fear on Flint's rugged face that his words should have caused. So he added, 'Or, if it doesn't happen, a certain sheriff may not be riding back to town.'

He flicked his gaze to The Major who smiled thinly and this time Macauley saw real fear flare wildly in the lawman's eyes.

Now that was more like it! Make sure they remember who's boss.

★ ★ ★

Reece Daimler cursed the rain that slashed at him and his two riders while they made their slow way through the hills. The tracks had led to this general area but they had arrived just a little too late to see where they continued because the rain had started, washing out the sign.

It was a real summer storm, hammering and driving down, even making the horses dance with its sting until they were led into the shelter of some trees. The men were drenched in minutes, but they shucked their slickers out of the dripping warbags and put them on anyway.

The rain was surprisingly cold and they rubbed and blew on wet hands. It was too wet to think of making cigarettes and they huddled in, cursing miserably under the trees. Reece Daimler was the most relaxed, being a man of the wilds. He dismounted and, holding his patched slicker tightly around his neck, moved to the edge of the trees. He squinted from beneath his sagging hat-brim.

'Reckon there'd be a cave of some sort up on that rim.'

'What's it matter?' growled one of the

men, Lindley, a handler from the freight store. 'We're wet as we can get already.'

'I wouldn't mind a fire,' allowed the second man, Lonnie Morton, son of the general-store keeper and used to his comforts. He was supposed to be a good shot.

Reece mounted again, saddle squelching as his weight settled. 'We'll go look — a fire sounds good. Anyone got a handful of coffee?'

Lindley owned up that he had and that decided it. They set out through the blinding rain, Reece leading in a zigzagging climb across a slope that was already washing away in parts, slippery and dangerous.

They made it all right, breath steaming along with the mounts', and at first they thought it had all been for nothing. No cave entrance was visible. But Reece dismounted, poked around amongst the big boulders and, behind a jumble of long-shattered shale, found a low entrance.

Rain was smashing off the rockface now, splashing into the air, and he gestured to the others to join him. They dismounted and led the protesting horses up, threaded a way through the rocks and lined up at the entrance.

Reece's nostrils were working and just as he was sure he smelled smoke and stale cooking, a gun began shooting from back in the darkness of the cave, flashes stabbing like orange daggers. Daimler spun, clutching at a searing pain streaking across his left hip. As he stumbled, fumbling for his sixgun under the wet slicker, Lindley cried out, choking on his own blood, his chest blown open in a gushing wound. He collapsed and Lonnie Morton dived for the ground. His Colt fell from his holster but was close beside him and he snatched it up instinctively. Stretched out on his belly, he began firing swiftly. The echoes boomed out at them, bullets whining and buzzing as they ricocheted from the rock walls.

'Judas! You'll kill us all with them

ricochets!' gritted Reece Daimler, his own gun in hand now.

'Long as I nail that sonuver in there!' gasped the excited Morton, his young heart hammering his ribs. His gun was empty now and Reece triggered two shots, low down, figuring whoever was in there would be lying prone.

He was right: a man grunted way back in the darkness, and there was no more gunfire. Lonnie was lying on his side, reloading, spilling more shells than he was stuffing into the chambers. Reece looked at him after examining Lindley and shook his head.

'Lin's dead — or will be in a coupla minutes. Slug tore him up good.'

'Or bad, dependin' on whether you're Lindley or not,' Morton said, snapping the Colt closed now. 'We goin' in . . . ?'

Daimler was already sliding in on his belly, feeling the warm blood from his hip soaking through his wet trousers. It was just beginning to hurt but he figured it couldn't be too bad. He paused as he saw a manshape lying slumped against the rear wall. There was a sixgun on the ground beside his limp hand. Reece took careful aim and fired a shot into the body. The man jerked and slumped to one side.

Lonnie had clapped his hands over his ears. 'Judas, Reece! Gimme some warnin' if you're gonna do that.'

Daimler looked at the dead man but it was too dark for identification. He could hear Lonnie Morton's teeth chattering.

'Better get some light in here. Gather up those old papers and I'll see if I can find a dry vesta in my pocket.'

'Papers might be important, Reece.'

'Hell, I can't read — they're covered with blood an' mud anyway.' He kicked some of the papers. 'Get a fire goin'. My nuts're freezin'.'

Lonnie nodded, holstered his sixgun, saw the dim shape of the papers and more spilling out of an open valise. He pulled them out, too, screwed them all into crumpled balls and rummaged around for twigs and dry leaves. There was a pile of kindling nearby.

'Looks like someone was stayin' here, Reece. Kindlin' and all, bit of hardtack an' so on. Dirty bandages, too.'

Daimler grunted, fumbling still for vestas. 'Ah! Couple of dry ones.' He scraped a match into flame and cupped a water-shrivelled hand around the flame as Lonnie held out a handful of crumpled papers, turning the edges so they caught fire almost instantly.

He dropped the flaming ball and pushed some kindling around it, feeding more paper in swiftly, flames beginning to roar as more were added. The cave was flickering with shadows and smoky, amber light. Kirk looked blankly across the small cave, his dead eyes not even reflecting the firelight.

* * *

Jericho, Hambone and Utah had been caught in the storm, too.

They rode into some brush under an

overhang of rock at the foot of the mountain slope. No one spoke, just huddled there in misery, waiting for the rain to stop or at least ease up.

'Ain't our day,' murmured Utah after a while.

Hambone shrugged but Jericho didn't even glance his way.

'Hush down!' he snapped and they saw his head was tilted in a listening attitude.

'What you hear, Jer?' Ham asked, and Jericho cussed him bitterly.

'Next thing *you* hear'll be my sixgun blowin' you outta the saddle!'

Ham sank in on himself, lower lip starting to pout at the rebuke. Jericho lifted a hand slowly, staring upslope, straining to hear. Utah heard it, too, and couldn't restrain himself from blurting out, 'Christ! Guns!'

Ward Jericho frowned, holding up a hand again for silence. 'Way up top.'

'Where our cave is!' Ham ventured the comment in a hushed voice.

'Damn posse!' Utah breathed.

'Must've found Kirk!'

'Likely so. Well, they ain't gonna find us! Let's get outta here! That hideout's finished for us.'

Jericho spurred his mount out from under the ledge's meagre protection and into the full onslaught of the rain.

'What — what about Kirk?' Ham asked.

'Kirk's done for,' Utah said. Jericho either didn't hear or couldn't be bothered to answer.

He kept riding through the rain, away from the mountainside now and into the heavier stands of timber. The other two followed, heads down against the lashing rain.

★   ★   ★

Cole Hardin was sitting on the porch of Glory Carnavan's ranch. She was standing in the doorway, watching the storm, visually checking the remuda in the corrals, the horses with enough savvy standing with their rumps turned to the rain. The barn door was banging, sagging from one hinge.

'I'll have to get Spud to fix that,' she murmured as if making a mental note.

'I've built barns,' Hardin told her. 'Be glad to fix anything round the place that needs a little carpentry.'

She smiled a little. 'Kind of you, Cole, but I don't think that arm of yours will stand the exercise just yet.'

He rubbed at the bandaged shoulder, the arm itself in a sling now: that had been at the girl's insistence.

'Gonna get more exercise than that soon as I can manage it,' he told her quietly, and at her quizzical look, added, 'It's my gun arm — can't afford to have it out of commission.' Out of the corner of his eye he saw her stiffen, turned to look up at her. 'That bother you?'

'It's your affair. You look hard, Cole, but not like a gunfighter.'

'Well, I wouldn't call myself *that*, but you got to know how to use a gun pretty good if you're on the drift these days.' He spoke a little curtly and she frowned slightly. 'Indians, wide-loopers, owlhoots . . . '

'Yes — of course.'

'I'll move out in a day or so.'

She laid a hand gently on his shoulder. 'I'm not telling you to do that. You won't be fit yet, despite what you may think.'

'How come you tended to me, Glory? Why didn't you turn me in to the posse?' Something else occurred to him then. 'You must've hidden the palomino, too. Flint would've seen it otherwise and asked some questions.'

'I think he was going to do just that, but the horse happened to be in the barn out of sight. In any case, the sheriff had barely arrived before someone came riding in to tell him about the train derailment. He turned and rode out with the posse almost straight away.'

Hardin nodded, still watching her. 'I'm obliged. And just for the record, I had nothing to do with that bank robbery — although I've known Ward Jericho on and off over the years.'

She smiled. 'When you've lived here for a while, you get to know Corey Flint and his habit of going off half-cocked. Spud picked up the story in town, how you came by the palomino and so on.'

'Yeah. Spud seemed concerned about this Silk.'

'Hi-spade Silk was a sleazy character. That palomino belonged to one of our neighbours, Magill, and Spud worked for him before he came here. Magill insisted that Silk had cheated him out of the horse and when Spud saw you riding it, he wondered if you were one of Silk's friends.'

'What happened to the palomino's original owner?'

She sobered, hesitated. 'The story is that Magill sulked over losing the horse, really pined for it, then got drunk enough one night to go after Silk. He was found dead in a back alley in town the next morning. Silk swore that he hadn't seen the man, and had some kind of suspect alibi.'

Hardin nodded. 'There was always that doubt, eh . . . ?'

'Always. Now Silk's dead and the horse has a good owner. Or, at least, I'd like to think so.'

'Me, too.'

'Well, perhaps you'll stick around long enough for us both to be sure.' She hesitated, then added, 'I can use another ranch hand — if you're interested.'

He turned to face her. 'Thanks, Glory, but, well, I still have my winnings from the poker game. They'll see me through a while before I need to hunt work.'

She regarded him soberly, then smiled a little. 'It must be a pretty good life just working when you need to, drifting around otherwise.'

He knew she was asking why he did it. 'I watched my old man work himself to death on a hardrock spread down in Comanche country, North Texas. Decided at an early age I wasn't gonna do that. There were five of us kids. Two died from sickness, weakened by malnutrition, I guess. The lung fever took my mother and the old feller went to pieces, turned into a drunk. My two sisters — ' He hesitated, lips tightening. 'Trish got married and I think she's tolerably happy, though worn down by six kids — she wouldn't be thirty yet. The other, well, Tilly was the looker of the family. She found out early on how to use those looks.'

He let it go at that and Glory had the decency not to ask him to explain further.

'After not having left the spread except to go into that rawhide town that served our needs for fourteen years, I rode out with a trail herd. Decided I was gonna be a cattle baron, have all the money I wanted and live an easy life.' He shrugged. 'Met a feller one day who just worked when he needed to, spent what he made on a good time, then found work again. He really enjoyed life, that feller, took me with him a couple of times. Gave me itchy feet but kinda made sense to me. Good sense.'

She could see how it would, coming from that harsh background. 'Well, I really could use an extra hand, Cole. I'm considering an offer from the Michigan and Western railroad for part of my land and I want my cattle rounded up and driven to market before they take over. I need the extra money the cattle will bring. I want to buy more land, back in the foothills, to make up for what I sell the railroad for their right-of-way.'

'Sounds like a good idea . . . OK, soon as my arm's in better shape, I'll stay a while. But no pay — don't argue about that, now, Glory! I always pay my debts and this one'll be a pleasure.'

Her smile warmed and widened.

'Yes, I believe it will.'

9

Workin' on the Railroad

They were a long way south now, trying to outrun the posse as well as the storm. But while they hadn't seen hide nor hair of Flint, the rain stayed with them until it finally started to clear of its own accord.

By that time they were all three drenched to the skin and shivering. Hambone found a deep overhang where a lot of leaves and twigs had collected over time. Tucked away back in a corner beside a bunch of bones and a few scraps of fur: the remains of an animal's birthing bed.

'Looks like Momma Puma whelped here,' Ham opined, collecting the dry, almost rotting wood.

'Long as she's long-gone,' allowed Utah.

'C'mon, hurry it up,' growled Jericho, briskly rubbing his arms and hands. 'We got coffee?'

They started a fire and brewed some coffee, holding their battered tin cups in both hands so as to draw a little extra warmth. They took off their clothes and spread them out where they could dry.

As the rain died, the wind died, too, and without its cutting bite they soon warmed up. They dried their tobacco and made cigarettes, enjoying the sensation of smoking, relaxing. 'Pretty good spot,' Ham allowed, looking for a compliment, but he was unsuccessful.

Utah grunted and Jericho swung his sober gaze across. 'Pretty good — for now. We got us a chore, boys. Have to find another good hole-in-the-wall. And I reckon we won't find one like that cave where we left Kirk.'

Utah shifted a little uneasily. 'He shoulda come with us.'

'Like hell! We'd be dead now or he'd've slowed us down so much the posse would've jumped us. An' I don't aim to have my neck stretched on no gallows. If we're cornered, I'm goin' down fightin'. A bullet's quicker'n a rope.'

That sobered them all and they were silent until the cigarettes had burned down so far as to singe their lips. They flicked the butts into the dying fire. Steam was rising from their clothes but there were a few dry patches showing. They were getting short of wood and Jericho figured the fuel would be all gone by the time their clothes were properly dry. He was feeling his shirt pockets, checking for vestas and maybe some more tobacco. His fingers located paper, and as he gingerly brought out the still-sodden folds, Utah said, 'Hell, we're flat broke now! After Delta and then missin' out on an express car on the train . . . we gotta find us a job to pull as well as a new hidey-hole, Jer.'

Jericho unfolded his paper. Both Utah and Hambone were surprised to see him grinning when he looked up.

He waved the damp paper. They

recognized it. 'Still got that railroad schedule,' Jericho said. 'Dry it out proper and gents, with a little luck, we won't be broke for long!'

★ ★ ★

Glory Carnavan was taking the vegetable scraps to the chicken pen when she saw the riders coming in out of the heatwaves shimmering between her ranch and the foothills. The mountain range was sharp and clear after the storm and heavy rain. The ground was drying out rapidly. Already the pastures were a brighter green, just two days since the storm had passed.

The herd was gathering: her crew, Spud, Stoke, Pedro and Crabb — and Hardin, too, despite her protests — were doing a good fast job of round up. If she could get the cows to market before the meat buyers returned to their packing houses, she would have a few thousand dollars extra in her hand. If she left the cattle for when the spread was sold to the rail-road, the buying season would be ended, so it was important that she get them to market quickly.

She had thought all was going along smoothly, but when she saw the riders, apprehension brought a small frown to her face.

It had to be the posse. Even from this distance she could pick out Corey Flint and that distinctive way he sat the saddle, almost as if one leg was slightly short, giving him a lean to the left. The man beside him in the cavalry hat could only be The Major. Hardin had described him when he had told her how the man had killed old Owl in cold blood.

Glancing out past the corrals, she saw two horse-men in the pasture where the herd was, bringing in strays to the main body; Spud and Stoke — Crabb was working on his mount's forefoot, under a tree near the forge, digging a stone out from under the shoe. Pedro? Ah, there! cornering two steers in a small draw, but where was Hardin?

Then the posse, looking haggard and weary, came into the yard, Flint touching a hand to his hat-brim as he looked around. 'Well, see you didn't get flooded, Glory.'

'We never do up on the rise here.' She ran her gaze along the ragged, weary men.

'Damn near drowned just ridin' along in that storm. Lost all hope of trackin' Jericho. Fisheye Creek cut us off all last night, had to swim it this mornin'. Glory, I gotta trouble you for some stores. We lost a couple pack mules in that damn creek.'

She frowned. 'Well, I'm fairly low, Corey, but I can find something to keep you going. Heading back to town?'

'No.' It was a sharp, curt answer, spoken by The Major. He looked at her in such a way as to make her uncomfortable, feeling that he was stripping her of her clothes. She felt her face flush hotly. 'We don't give up that easy, lady.' He looked steadily at Flint. 'Do we, Sheriff?'

'No. Guess not.' Flint sounded surly. 'Well, we'll take what you can spare, Glory.' He swivelled to look at The Major. 'Guess we're gonna be ridin' for some time yet.'

'For as long as it takes, Flint. You know Mr Macauley wants Jericho and his bunch caught.'

Glory saw the hostility between the men and opened her mouth to reply when there came a series of distant popping sounds from the foothills. The Major straightened in the saddle, hipped swiftly. 'That's gunfire!'

Flint frowned, seemed uncertain what to do for a moment, then said, 'You know anythin' about it, Glory?'

'I — I think it's one of my cowhands — practising.'

'What kind of cowhands you hiring, lady?' The Major asked tightly.

'Wouldn't be that Hardin, would it?' Flint asked, showing more perception than the girl would have given him credit for.

There was no use lying. 'He's been

wounded and is recovering — '

'Exercising his gun-arm!' The Major said, mind on only one thing. 'Where? C'mon, woman! Where'll we find him?'

'Sounds to me like it's comin' from that bottleneck draw you got t'other side of the hogback.' Flint's face was grim now and The Major wheeled his mount and spurred away in the direction the sheriff had indicated. Flint smothered a curse. 'Damn! Tully, you come with me. Rest of you get washed up at the pump and pack them stores Glory's gonna give us.'

She could have bitten her tongue but it was too late now . . .

★ ★ ★

The Major dismounted when he saw the entrance to the draw. The palomino was ground-hitched on a patch of fresh young grass and he drew his sixgun as he leapt from the saddle and went in at a crouch.

A volley of gunshots roared up the

draw and he winced as they thunder-clapped his ears. Easing up to a rock, he looked around it and saw Hardin, sling hanging loosely from his neck, massaging his right upper arm, a smoking sixgun held down at his side. The Major stayed put, watched Hardin reload, holster his gun and flex the fingers of his right hand. He shrugged the shoulder and it moved a little stiffly.

Then the Peacemaker was blazing in his fist and four of the six apple-sized rocks lined up on a dead-fall about twenty paces away disintegrated into dust and rock chips. As Hardin shucked out the spent shells, The Major smiled thinly to himself and triggered twice, so fast it was almost like a single shot. The two remaining untouched rocks exploded in puffs of dust and then Hardin was crouching, one cartridge only in the chamber as he snapped the cylinder closed and cocked the hammer, gun barrel steady on the intruder.

The speed startled the killer and he

was caught with his own gun pointing halfway to the ground. 'My God! Why the hell're you practising when you can move that fast?'

Hardin's eyes were narrowed. His shoulder was burning, tight with fierce pain from the hour or so's practice he had already put in. But he willed his gun not to waver or tremble and so expose this weakness. 'There's always someone faster.'

The Major snorted. 'You believe that?'

'Seen it happen over and over. Clay Nash in Deadwood. Ben Bridges in Sioux Falls. Chap O'Keefe in White Cloud — all *bueno hombres* and fast guns, but they knew some day they'll meet someone faster. I know it, too.'

'Well, sure, I'm faster'n you. But I don't figure there's anyone faster'n me.'

'Be too late by the time you find out for sure.'

The Major smiled crookedly. 'Reckon you'll be dead by then.'

'Could be.' Hardin hesitated, then

snapped out the cylinder and completed his reloading. He looked up. 'You're kinda quick with that damn rifle, too.'

The Major grinned. 'That old Indian? Did him a favour, sending him to the Happy Hunting Grounds.'

Hardin was about to answer, but hastily closed the gun cylinder as he heard riders in the draw entrance. Then Flint and Tully suddenly appeared, rifles out. The sheriff covered Hardin, his Winchester cocked and aimed.

'Been wantin' to talk with you.'

'Ain't mutual, Sheriff.'

'Well, now, you don't have no choice, Hardin. We'll go on back to Glory's. She's got some talkin' to do, too.'

★　★　★

'You could've told me he was here the other day when we rode in, Glory.'

Flint's voice was cold and he sounded peeved. His posse, pack mule now loaded with Glory's stores, sat their mounts in

169

a half circle around the porch. The Major was impatient and stared in that cold, embarrassing way at the girl.

She gave her attention to the lawman. 'There wasn't really time, Corey. You were hardly reined-down when that rider came in with news about the train derailment . . . it seemed more urgent than me telling you a strange wounded man was lying in the barn.'

Flint frowned, couldn't find a reasonable argument and finally nodded, turning to Hardin. 'I've been back to town to form up this new posse and I guess I'll have to allow your meetin' with Jericho was just one of them things.'

Hardin had nothing to add: he was all through trying to convince Flint of his innocence.

'So right now I'll give you the benefit of the doubt, but, Glory, I want you to keep him here till I get back.'

'We're rounding up for a trail drive to the railhead at the tanks, Sheriff. I'll need Cole for that.'

His frown deepened. 'Kinda late in

the season for a drive that far.'

'I need the money.'

When it was apparent she was not going to say more, Flint shrugged. 'OK, men, we'll ride on.'

'Why don't we take Hardin along?' The Major said with something of a leer as he looked at the drifter. 'He seems to be a good tracker.'

'Old Owl got me as far as we went before,' Hardin said quickly. 'It was nothing I did.' He rubbed his arm absently and The Major scoffed.

'You're not gonna claim that wound's bothering you? Not after the way you used that six-shooter.'

'It bothers me. But I have a job here and you've a whole slew of men, Sheriff. You don't need one more.'

Flint shook his head. 'I got enough worries without draggin' a wounded man along as well, Major.'

The gunfighter didn't even argue. It had apparently just been a pointless niggle that Hardin had taken in his stride. But maybe that told The Major something more about this man he had a hunch he would be meeting over a smoking gun in the not too distant future.

As the posse rode out of the yard, Glory said soberly, 'I think that man, The Major, is interested in you, Cole.'

He nodded slightly. 'Yeah, he saw me shoot, reckons he's faster on the draw — but his kind have to put it to the test and make sure.'

She looked alarmed. 'You think he'll challenge you?'

'Sure.'

'And it doesn't bother you?'

'Sure it does, but it'll happen. Nothing I can do about it.'

Her white teeth tugged at her full lower lip and her hands involuntarily twisted her apron-front.

* * *

The locomotive panted like an asthmatic old man, slowly and heavily, the cow-catcher barely two yards from the newly felled tree blocking the tracks.

Utah sat his horse there, a shotgun aimed into the cab where the engineer and his sidekick stood, tensed and pale. He could hear the mild screams of some of the women passengers in the car just behind the coal tender as they were relieved of their purses. He glanced along the train past the freight wagons to the express car just before the caboose.

It was easy to get the shotgun guards to open the door of the car. All Jericho did was drag an old couple from the train, stand them where the guards could see through their eye-slits cut into the reinforced timber, and place his cocked sixgun against the trembling old lady's silver hair.

'Open the door, gents, or she dies. Then the old feller and, hell, if you're still playin' dumb I can work my way through the whole damn passenger car.' His voice hardened. 'And you know damn well I ain't bluffin'.'

The guards knew. They tossed their

guns out a small window and then slid back the door. Jericho had to shoot one of the guards before the other produced the hidden key to the strongbox. The man was shaking, middle-aged and likely had a family, sure he was going to be killed.

But Ward Jericho liked to do the unexpected and he took the man back to the caboose where the train guard was already trussed up like a Sunday turkey.

He was an oldster, too, on his last run for the railroad before retirement, he claimed. He strained to look up as Jericho bound the express-car guard on the floor beside him. 'Least you ain't runnin' the train off no cliff.'

'Don't happen to be one handy.'

The train guard snorted. 'Hell, you derail a passenger train and you'll never rest easy again! Whole country'll be after your hide.'

Jericho casually backhanded him, bringing a bead of blood to his leathery old lips.

'Leave him be,' growled the guard, struggling instinctively against his bonds.

'Judas, you don't appreciate nothin' do you? Here I do you a favour an' tie you up instead of shootin' you and you gimme a mouthful of lip! Ah, the hell with you!'

He drew his sixgun and shot the man in the head. The old man started to gag, struggling to get away from the twitching body beside him. His rheumy eyes were full of fear now. Jericho seemed to be making some sort of decision and abruptly holstered his gun. Hambone came panting up to the door. 'All OK, Jer?'

Jericho stood. 'Yeah, just the express guard bein' sassy, and the old man tellin' me we better not derail a passenger train or the whole damn world'll be after us. Takes all the fun outta it, when you gotta get real serious.'

Hambone gave his rooster call and grinned inanely, saying, 'Man, I bet that railroad'd have a fit we derailed a passenger train!'

Jericho nodded absently, tossed the canvas money-sack from the express car to Hambone and began reloading his Colt. They walked on down the train to where Utah waited with the mounts. Then Jericho suddenly stopped in his tracks, startling Hambone.

'Yeah! The railroad'd sure be mighty upset we start derailin' their trains. They might even be willin' to pay us not to bother 'em!'

Hambone blinked. 'Pay us?'

Jericho nodded, half-smiling now. 'Damn right! What you reckon it'd be worth to 'em for us not to hit their trains . . . mebbe $10,000 a time? And no risk to us!'

'Where you goin', Jer?' Utah called as the man swung aboard the car where the newly robbed passengers still cowered.

'Gotta be someone here who can write proper and spell the right words . . . ' He paused at the top of the

176

steps, one hand holding the brass rail, the other his sixgun. 'We got us a letter to write! With a little luck, we'll be workin' for the railroad — by *not doin' one goddam thing*!'

10

Cold Cash

The posse stayed out another two days, going south all the time. Then, when they called into a stage swing-station at Marlowe's Creek for a change of mounts, they were given startling news.

Mendez, the half-Mexican station manager, didn't want to hand over his horses. He was a tubby man, his skin greasy because he sweated a lot, this brought about because he was a hard worker. He used Indians, sometimes a couple of hardcase whites looking for a few dollars, to work the station which served stages both northbound and southbound. So there was constant work and sometimes the changeover teams hardly had a chance to rest up before they were due to be put back into harness again on the next stage through.

'I got a man up in the hills right now, tryin' to trap mustangs so's we can break 'em and add to the remuda, Sheriff,' Mendez told Flint.

'Good, you oughta have 'em in by the time the next stage is due. We'll take what's in the corrals.'

'No you won't, Sheriff. This station ain't even in your bailiwick and I ain't obliged to help you.'

Flint frowned. 'You always helped before, Mendez.'

'Sure, when you had only one or two men, but how many you got now? Ten? Twelve? You'll clean me out. No, my first obligation is to the company.'

'Hell, I'll sign a chit to pay for 'em!'

Mendez sighed, wiped his face with a grimy rag and shook his head. 'You don't savvy, Corey. It ain't the money! It's the hosses I got available. I let you take what's in the corrals, I won't have a spare team broke from the mustangs before the southbound comes through.

Be more'n my job's worth to cause a delay like that.'

The Major shouldered Flint aside and towered above the short Mexican. 'Could be more'n your *life's* worth, 'breed.'

Mendez was no fool. He looked at this man and felt a rush of fear but he tried to cover — not too well. '*Señor*, I have been a loyal employee of the Continental Divide Stageline for ten years and I — '

He stopped as The Major's sixgun whispered out of leather and the muzzle pressed up under his fatrolled chin. He shuddered and felt an urge to empty his bladder as the gun hammer notched back.

'Easy, Major! Easy!' Flint said quickly. 'Judas, we don't need to do this!'

'We do. Mr Macauley wants Jericho caught and quickly. No time to fool around with this greaser — is there, Mendez?' He screwed the muzzle deep into the sweaty roll of fat and the foresight dug in and scraped the flesh raw. Mendez squirmed, eyes rolling, silently pleading with the sheriff.

'Jericho?' he managed to gasp. 'I — I got a telegraph — about him . . . '

The Major frowned and shook Mendez. 'The hell you say!'

Released momentarily, the Mexican rubbed the under side of his jaw where there was a little blood mixing with the sweat now. He nodded vigorously. 'It's for someone named Hunsecker — '

'No one of that name in this posse,' Flint said, 'But we'll — '

'I'm Hunsecker,' snapped The Major. 'Get the wire!'

Flint watched The Major as Mendez hurried back into the station's main building. There was a small telegraph office there, Mendez himself working it as part of his duties.

'Didn't know your name,' the sheriff said, but The Major ignored him, snatched the yellow form that Mendez brought back.

He read swiftly, swore softly, looking bleakly at the lawman. 'We need to return at once to Wildwood.'

'What? Who the hell says so?'

'I say so.' The Major was truculent, waiting for a protest. Then he added, 'Mr Macauley's had word from railroad headquarters. Jericho's made some demands and, well, that's all it says, but we have to get back as quick as we can.'

Mendez started to relax. The quicker the better, he told himself, but he kept his usual sad expression, while inwardly he rejoiced.

But not for long.

Suddenly, The Major turned on him, sixgun blasting, and Mendez screamed as the bullet smashed his right knee cap. He collapsed, writhing in the dust, blood spurting between his clasping fingers, face contorted. 'Next time don't argue with your betters, greaser.'

Flint snapped, 'Goddamnit! No need for that!'

'Get fresh horses,' The Major said, and the suddenly silent possemen moved swiftly towards the corrals. 'Flint, just accept that I am in charge here. You and the others will do like I say — exactly like I say! If you have any complaints, take them up with Mr Macauley.' Then his mouth lifted at one corner in a crooked smile. 'He'll no doubt pass them along to me to deal with.'

Flint could see there would be little use to argue here. In fact, it could be downright fatal.

'One other thing,' The Major added casually, but still with that crooked smile. 'We need to stop at the woman's place.'

Flint frowned. 'Glory Carnavan's?'

'Yes, Mr Macauley wants us to bring in the drifter, Hardin.'

★　★　★

There wasn't much Cole Hardin could do when the posse rode in and demanded he return to Wildwood with them.

'Why?'

The Major demonstrated his fast

draw — and it was fast, like a streak of lightning but much smoother. He waved the Colt briefly. 'This reason enough?'

'Could be.'

'Cole, will you be all right?' The girl looked and sounded concerned.

'Course he'll be all right,' The Major said, leaning out of the saddle and lifting Hardin's Colt from its holster. 'Been practising since I last saw you, drifter?'

'Every day.'

'Improved, I hope.'

'About as good as I ever was.'

'Is that all? Shoulder healing?'

'Pretty much.'

'Good, maybe we'll see just how good you are. Now let's move! We've some hard riding ahead. Oh, Hardin. You'll be riding your palomino, I take it?'

Cole nodded.

'Good.'

And on that puzzling note the posse rode out, leaving Glory Carnavan and

Spud staring after them.

'I think I better ride into town, too,' the girl said quietly.

'Want me along, ma'am?'

She shook her head. 'You and the crew carry on, Spud, bring down the rest of the cattle from the hills. I need to get in touch with one of the meat agents but I'll be back as soon as I can and we'll get the drive started.'

* * *

The meeting was held in Borden's office and it was mighty crowded. There was Borden, of course, Macauley, The Major, Corey Flint and Cole Hardin. Only Borden and Macauley were seated. Macauley studied Hardin's lean form as the man leaned against the wall, left hand massaging his right shoulder. His holster was empty, his sixgun on the end of Borden's desk where The Major had left it. He kept his eye on the weapon as Macauley began to speak.

'No time for beating around the bush. Hardin, we want you to deliver something for us. You'll be paid well. How does a hundred dollars sound?'

'Like it's not all that much, depending on what I have to do.'

Macauley narrowed his eyes and the banker, showing obvious signs of nervousness, said, 'We may dicker a little but we won't waste time. We want you to deliver a certain package . . . to Ward Jericho.'

Hardin stiffened and he saw Flint was just as surprised as he was. The Major narrowed his own eyes and Hardin had the notion that this was the first the man had heard any details of this deal, too.

'What is it?' the drifter asked quietly. 'Pay-off money?'

'It's blackmail!' snapped Macauley, and it was clear he was seething inside. 'Something we cannot avoid, and I don't mind telling you it riles the insides out of me!'

'How much?' Hardin asked. The

banker and Macauley exchanged a look and the latter shook his head.

'You don't need to know.'

'The hell I don't, Mister. I'm in the driving seat here, for a while at least. You want me to do this chore, you not only pay me a decent fee, you give me all the details. It's my neck on the block.'

The Major rounded on him fast, hand slapping gun butt. He staggered across the room as Hardin's left shoulder rammed into him and when he straightened he froze, gun half-drawn, looking down the muzzle of Hardin's Colt which he had snatched off the desk. Air whistled softly through Flint's bared teeth.

'If you're faster'n that, Major, I sure as hell want to see it!'

The Major's face tightened and a kind of mad look made his eyes murky. 'You'll see it.' His words were barely audible. 'At the right time. You can damn well bet on that!'

'Give your ego a rest,' Hardin told

him, looking now at Macauley. 'You'd best start talking, mister. I get the notion this is kind of urgent . . . '

★　★　★

Ward Jericho had gotten meaner since Hardin had known him riding shotgun for the stages.

Wrecking that freight train, killing all six crewmen on board, was one thing. Holding up the passenger-freight train on the Black Canyon line was another. The caboose guard had told how Jericho had murdered one of the guards in cold blood and threatened to shoot a passenger's wife unless the man wrote out his demands to be forwarded to the railroad company, the Michigan and Western Line.

These same demands had been passed on to Macauley to be dealt with. Jericho had learned since that Macauley was a field agent for the railroad, travelled all over, mostly with The Major, straightening out any problems, making deals on land required for right-of-way. A kind of trouble-shooter which gave him plenty of opportunities to know the company's innermost secrets . . . and turn them to his own advantage.

What Jericho didn't know about Macauley was that he also serviced The Group, a tight-knit band of hard-headed, ruthless financiers who used his position to keep tabs on the railroads and their rapid expansion. With Macauley's information and sometimes physical help, they obtained advance insight into plans for new extensions, manipulated the share market on both land and industry — for expansion meant new track and The Group had vested interests in iron and steel foundries, timber for carriage-making, coal mines for fuel.

The Major was also one of their men, though ostensibly he worked only for Macauley and the railroad the man represented. Macauley was sweating blood that this deal would come off: if

Jericho was allowed to carry out his threats and the railroad changed its mind about using this location, then The Group stood to lose huge funds already heavily invested.

And they were bad losers . . .

Still, this latest development seemed straightforward enough.

Jericho had simply given the railroad company a choice: pay him $10,000 or he would wreck the next train he robbed. It would be a passenger train and they would never know where or when until it happened. Pay him the money and he would leave them in peace.

Until he spent the $10,000 and wanted more.

That, of course, was not stated but everyone knew it would happen.

And his final demand had been that the delivery be made by Cole Hardin — riding the palomino.

Hardin knew it was his death warrant. Jericho held a grudge forever and he apparently was mad at Hardin for having won the palomino from Silk and then taking back the horse from him, Jericho, after he had lifted the animal for the bank robbery getaway.

He would be riled that Hardin had led the posse to his favourite stronghold — even if done inadvertently — and now he saw his chance to square things. Get Hardin to bring the $10,000, shoot him and take back the palomino all in one.

Hardin had asked for $1,000 to make the delivery and that had caused some spirited discussion between Borden, Macauley and Hardin. The Major had waited for Macauley to give him a signal to kill Hardin on the spot but they were too desperate and pushed for time. So they agreed.

There was a train already on the way that contained a whole theatre troupe that was very popular throughout the country, back East as well as on the Frontier. The so-called 'Carolina Song-stress' — singer and dancer Beatrice 'Babe' DeLarue — was with the troupe.

If anything happened to her, well, the company might just as well wrap up business. No one would ever ride a Michigan and Western Line train again.

There was no guarantee that this particular train would be Jericho's next target but it would be on the schedule he had. The man was smart as well as ruthless, and once he knew it was already travelling he would be bound to set his sights for it.

Even the cold-eyed Macauley showed signs of nervousness when early negotiations had looked like breaking down or being prolonged. He wanted this deal over and done with, pronto, but he bitterly resented having no choice but to give in to Jericho's demands.

It was made clear to Hardin: comply, or be thrown into jail on trumped-up charges that could eventually see him on a high gallows. Or, maybe, The Major had added slyly, someone might even shoot him through the barred cell window some dark night before the hangman arrived . . .

Hardin had seen half the thousand dollar fee paid into an account that Borden had opened for him and Flint had insisted on riding as far as the foothills with him.

'That's a heap of money you've got there, drifter, and it better be delivered to Jericho. You savvy? You'll never get away with keepin' it for yourself.'

Hardin smiled thinly. 'Difference between you and me, Flint — I never even considered not delivering it.'

The sheriff flushed. 'So you say! But listen, Hardin, there's a good chance you won't come out of this alive.'

'I know.'

'A thousand bucks all you figure your life's worth?'

Hardin shrugged. 'I'm a bit of a gambler, Flint, you know that. Besides, I saw Babe De Larue at the Canary Theatre in Tombstone once. Wouldn't want anything to happen to her.'

Flint shook his head, scratched at his stubble. 'You're *loco*, Hardin, you know that?'

'It's been said. Might see you when I get back if I head down this way again. Could even afford to buy you a drink.'

'I wouldn't bother . . . '

And now here he was, following the trail Jericho had worked out, tensed and alert. He wouldn't put it past the outlaw to jump him somewhere along the way, long before he reached the draw near Manitou Pass where the money was supposed to be paid over.

It was a good choice for the deal: the walls of the pass were high and gave a clear, unobstructed view across the flats in both the approaches to the pass. Once paid, the outlaws could slip away into the hills within a short, hard ride, and, with Jericho knowing the country as well as he did, they might never be seen nor heard of again.

Except they would be: Hardin knew Jericho wouldn't keep his word. Oh, sure, he might let the train carrying the theatre troupe through, but there would be other passenger trains and the company would feel obliged to pay 'protection' money again and again so they could proceed safely. They would be hunted relentlessly but, with some luck, and Jericho's innate cunning, he could be a rich man in a few months.

And *Hardin* could be dead within a few minutes if he allowed his mind to wander like this . . .

He had no sooner brought his full attention back to the trail than two riders appeared out of the brush a few yards ahead. And even as he slowed the palomino he heard another horse behind him and recognized Jericho's laugh as the man said, 'You always was right on time, Cole! Remember tellin' you once it'd be the death of you.'

He heard a gun hammer click back to full cock.

11

Double Cross

Hardin didn't hesitate. He knew he was a breath away from death and pitched sideways out of the saddle. It was a narrow trail, winding high into the hills, and only a brush-choked ravine was below him now. As he left the startled palomino, he snatched the rifle together with its scabbard, hoping the rawhide thongs that held it to the saddle-flap would snap.

They did, hanging up only briefly. But even that small split-second delay jarred his body off the line he had intended to take. And just as well! Jericho, always a fast thinker, had seen Hardin's move — it had been not altogether unexpected — and swung his gun into the intended arc. He fired and the bullet tore and rattled through swaying brush below, missing Hardin's hurtling body by a foot.

The drifter dropped and by the time he crashed into the cushioning brush, Jericho was shooting again, as were Hambone and Utah from the front. He twisted so as to land on his back, feeling the twigs and slim branches tear at his clothing, each with a tentative, fleeting grip, but all the time slowing his fall, even if only minutely. An arm across his face protected his eyes and then the bushes thickened and heavier branches battered him until he landed on the ground with a great gusting out-breathing and a jar that rattled his teeth.

He dropped the rifle but lunged after it as it fell away down a slope that was a hell of a lot steeper than it had looked in that flashing instant before he had dived off the horse. Bullets tore and whipped all round, spitting gravel and dust, small twigs flying, stinging when they touched exposed flesh. Somehow his hand closed over the skidding Winchester — the end of the barrel — and the foresight tore a groove across his palm before he tightened his grip.

His heels caught on some obstruction and he yelled involuntarily as his body snapped erect as if on a spring, tearing up through the screening bushes. He was exposed from the waist up for a couple of seconds before crashing back under. He jerked as lead seared across his neck. By now he had the rifle in both hands, raised it horizontally in front of him and used it like a battering ram as he continued to fall.

He was not in control by a long way. His body arced one moment, was flung straight like a ramrod the next, curled around a sapling, leaves stripping from the flexible branches as he grabbed frantically for something to slow this damn dangerous downhill slide.

A volley from above raked the area where he was headed but they were anticipating too much, shot too far ahead. With a mighty effort that wrenched his almost-healed shoulder, he managed to twist and fling himself to one side.

He stopped with a jolt and felt something hit him across the bridge of the nose. Warm blood spurted from his nostrils and his vision went crazy for a few moments as the top of his skull seemed to fly off. They were still shooting from the high trail as if bullets were a dime a hundred. Suddenly the guns stopped, the echoes dying away, silence gradually creeping into the deep ravine once more.

Hardin was in deep shadow down here and lay still as a dead possum, one scratched and bleeding hand wrapped tightly around the rifle's barrel. He could just make out voices from above.

'We nail him, Jer?'

'How the hell do I know? Can't tell with all that brush, but he's sure deep down. Even if we didn't weigh him down with a couple pounds of lead, reckon he'll have one helluva job climbin' back up this side of Sunday week.'

'We gonna wait an' see?' The cautious Utah again.

'You can if you want. Me, I'm lightin' out on my brand new palomino with a poke full of *dinero*. To hell with Hardin. I've got what I want.'

Though semi-conscious, Hardin heard the brief laughter and Utah say, emphatically, 'Damn right! I'm with you, Jer!'

Then the crowing of a rooster drifted down into the ravine, briefly silencing the insects that had started up. Soon, their renewed buzzings and sawings and clickings were the only sounds to be heard, apart from a distant birdsong high above.

* * *

'Goddamn, I knew it! I knew that lousy drifter wouldn't show like he was s'posed to!'

Sheriff Corey Flint was purple-faced with rage and his clenched fist slammed down on to the saddlehorn. It hurt like blazes but damned if he was going to let it show now in front of The Major and the rest of the posse.

They were in the trees on the rim above the small draw that Jericho had named as the pick-up place for the $10,000. Flint, urged on by Macauley and Borden, had come here, riding most of the night before so as to get ahead of Hardin, the courier.

The posse had cold-camped, and Flint had forbidden smoking: nothing must alarm the outlaws if they arrived early. Also, he didn't want Hardin to know he was being watched.

'Hardin isn't the only one who hasn't showed,' The Major said bluntly.

Flint looked at him through the shade here among the trees and dropped his gaze down into the draw where the shadows were deeper. 'No-o. I guess Jericho ain't managed to sneak in without us seein' him. He might aim to let Hardin bring the money, stash it where he said, among the roots of that old ponderosa stump, and then collect later.'

The Major's face was scornful. 'What d'you use for brains, Flint? D'you think Jericho specially asked that Hardin make the delivery because he just wants to pick up the money? Dammit, man, he's after the palomino *at least*! My bet is he aims to square away with Hardin, too, for some grudge he holds. There's not much chance Hardin would ride away from this draw. Not if Jericho was waiting for him.'

Flint swallowed his anger at the man's insulting tone. 'You sound as if you figure Jericho won't show at all!'

'Does it make sense to you that he wouldn't be here waiting for Hardin and the money?'

'No. That's what I'm sayin'. He ain't here yet — '

'Because he never intended to be!' cut in The Major, voice harsh-edged now. He watched Flint blink. 'You getting it yet, you dummy? *Jericho never meant for Hardin to bring the money here!* He was waiting some-where along the trail and has jumped Hardin, killed him, I guess, and taken the money already . . . Christ, a five-year-old can work that out.'

Flint had had enough. 'Then how come it took you so long? Look, I've had a bellyful of your insults, Major. You don't scare me.'

'Well, you're a bigger fool than I thought, Flint. You *ought* to be scared of me! Because Mr Macauley don't have no more use for you now. You're too damn dumb!'

Flint was way too slow: too slow figuring out just what The Major was saying, too slow in trying to bring up the rifle he held across his saddle, and way too slow to dodge the two bullets that smashed into his chest and knocked him spinning off his horse.

The Major sat his mount calmly, smoking gun in hand, watching to make sure there wasn't even a twitch of life left in the sheriff.

And suddenly he heard the clatter of

hoofs behind him, spun in the saddle in time to see the posse scattering amongst the trees, dodging the shadowed trunks and low slung branches. Raging at being caught off-guard, The Major emptied his Colt after them. Bullets whined and chewed bark from the trunks but he knew he hadn't hit anyone. He started to reach for the big Henry but checked the movement. To hell with it anyway. He'd done the job he was supposed to. He reloaded the Colt quickly, looked around, only briefly at the dead sheriff, then unshipped the Henry anyway. He felt better just holding the big gun.

And he needed some sort of comfort because he had to find his way out of here now. Contemptuous of Flint and thinking out just how and when he would kill the man as Macauley had ordered, he hadn't bothered watching the trail up there. Just followed these possemen he considered far beneath him in intellect and everything else.

Now — he hated to admit it even to himself — he was close to being as lost as he had ever been.

* * *

They had come far along the trail leading to the hideout they now frequented in the hills, not far from Manitou Pass.

It had been a gruelling ride, skirting the pass where they knew the posse would likely be waiting, hoping to jump them when they picked up the money. But Jericho was in a pretty good mood. He had the palamino and $10,000. Hardin was out of commission for quite a while, maybe permanently.

And they were riding free. All they had to do now was keep on going south, cross into New Mexico and head on down to Santa Fe and whip the town into shape with a wingding they would talk about for years afterward.

But even $10,000 wouldn't last for ever.

Not when it had to be split three ways . . .

They were at the start of a precarious, winding narrow trail here and Jericho hauled rein, bringing the palomino's head up with a jerk. The others stopped suddenly, too. Hambone gentled his horse, looking at Jericho, who seemed worried. 'What's up, Jer?'

'Hardin bothers me. We should've made sure we put a couple shots into him. I know him from the old days. Once a stage went off a high trail and he climbed a cliff that was almost straight up, then ran seven miles back to the swing-station for help.'

'You said it'd take him a week to get outta that ravine,' Utah reminded him.

Jericho nodded, making his frown deeper. 'I know, but can't shake the hunch he might just make it out. Ham, you ride back an' watch that trail where he went over. If there's movement down there, empty your gun at it. If you see Hardin make damn sure you kill the son of a bitch.'

Ham frowned, absorbing the brief orders. He nodded: it didn't make much sense to him, but he knew he wasn't as smart as Jericho, not even Utah. 'What about my money, Jer?'

'Hell, it's safe.' Jericho rapped the canvas bank sack with its padlocked leather collar slung from the palomino's saddlehorn. 'We'll keep it for you, up at the hideout. Give it till sundown tomorrow before you start back, OK? You got it, Ham, what I want you to do . . . ?'

Ham grinned and gave his rooster crow. 'I got it, Jer!' He started to turn his mount and then paused. 'Will I be back in time to see that train jump the rails?'

'Hell, yeah, I reckon so. Utah and me won't even prise the bolts outta the ties till you come. We can find ourselves a nice shady tree on the hillside and watch that loco jump the bend like a stone shot from a catapult.' He grinned. 'Might even hear that songbird give a last scream! Kind of a free performance just for us, eh?'

Ham grinned and rode away. Utah looked thoughtful.

'We really gonna derail that train after all?'

'Why not? Kind of a last gesture, a reminder it could happen any time! And next time we'll ask for $20,000 — and they'll pay!'

'You got a head on you, Jer, I'll give you that, but Ham might not be back in time — ' He broke off when he saw Jericho's face, the man's amused, crooked smile. 'Oh-oh!'

'Don't worry about Ham. Two-way split sounds better'n three-way, don't it?'

Utah nodded slowly. It did, but . . .

As they rode on he couldn't help wonder if Jericho was already figuring no split was by far the best way of all.

★ ★ ★

Hardin was lucky: he had no broken bones, only some bruising and bumps and his clothes looked like a scare-crow's. But he was all in one piece and he still held his rifle. Now all he had to do was find a way out of here.

It would be one hell of a climb, he decided, parting the brush so as to see better. Actually, he couldn't see the trail up there. He would have to back up a way before he could do that. But he knew it was too steep to climb up there: he would have to find another way out.

Not knowing the country was a distinct disadvantage. He smashed a path through the heavy brush with the butt of the Winchester, his shoulder throbbing, but not bleeding. He felt the ground start to lift a little under his badly scuffed boots. Pausing, he could see the brush and timber rising so he continued until he figured the elevation was as high as it was going to go. There was a slim pine some twenty feet high, and he managed to jump up and catch the lowest branch. He swung himself up and used the branches like a step ladder to climb higher.

The trail he had left so dramatically was dauntingly high and he was more convinced than ever that he would be unable to climb such a vertical cliff. He looked around very slowly, examining the rise and fall of the vegetation, slipped once and tore skin from his hand on the rough bark as he grabbed frantically, legs dangling in space. But after righting himself, he found he was facing in a direction he had not yet examined — and he saw his way out.

The ravine sides sloped down sharply just around the bend from where he had jumped from the palomino. He glimpsed a section of foothills with scant brush and trees, way beyond.

Hardin climbed down carefully, retrieved the rifle he had propped against the pine's base and took his bearings.

Then he started walking. 'Inching' might be a better description, for he had to batter a way through the entangled scrub and pause frequently to look up through the overhead branches and leaves to make sure he was still headed in the right direction.

Heat and thirst plagued him rapidly but there was no sign of water even though the vegetation was so thick. It must have been all underground and he had neither energy nor time to dig. He wanted to be out of here before sundown. Already the insects were driving him crazy, buzzing and biting, filling his ears and nostrils, the corners of his eyes, on his neck, especially where the bullet had seared the skin.

His arms were aching, his shoulder burning like someone was holding a branding-iron against it. His legs were leaden: walking was top of the list as one of the most-hated things any cowboy had to do. Riding boots weren't meant for terrain like this and the rifle was suffering abuse, being used like a club to force a way through the scrub.

He felt a twitch of worry as he saw the sun heeling over towards the west. If he didn't get out of here by nightfall, the bugs would eat him alive, or his eyes would swell up from bites so he couldn't see. Not to mention thirst and hunger further incapacitating him.

He stopped when he realized he was slamming and swinging the rifle harder and more frequently than he needed to, forced himself to take a five-minute rest. His tobacco sack was damp with sweat in his shirt pocket but he found enough dry weed to roll a smoke and light it. It tasted good, but he knew it would only make his thirst worse. Still, a small mercy was exactly that. So he truly enjoyed the cigarette before starting off again.

He wasn't too sure he was still heading in the right direction, but the angle of the sun seemed right, as in relation to himself, the touch of its rays occasionally on his face, when it penetrated the branches and leaves pretty much where they should be. There was no choice, anyway.

So, rubbing his fingertips over the freshly scarred and dented rifle stock, he used the heavy octagonal barrel to batter aside obstructing brush. He reckoned this must have been one of the longest days of his life.

But it ended in mid-to-late afternoon when he finally burst through screening bushes and found himself in a small clearing, bare grass and stunted, scattered brush giving way to a stand of timber.

The trees were filling with birds, their mingled chirpings and calls telling him this was probably an evening watering place. The knowledge lent power to the screaming muscles of his legs and he stumbled forward, into the cool shade of the timber, plunged through recklessly, the noise of his passage sending clouds of whirling birds screeching their protest from the higher branches.

And there was the pool. Dark water, the surface speckled with beetles and dragonflies and dead leaves and bits of twigs. He parted this scum with his shaking hands and plunged his face under. It tasted better than any drink he could remember. Scooping up hatfuls, he poured it over himself, luxuriating in its coolness, refreshing his tortured body. He couldn't hope to get back to Wildwood, or even Glory Carnavan's, before dark so he started to scoop up layers of dead leaves to make a bed for the night.

It was almost finished when the first shot shattered the sundown peace — although the birds were still calling — and leaves and detritus erupted into his face. Instinct took over. Hardin threw himself backwards, snatching up the ill-treated Winchester as he went.

Two more rapid shots zipped and buzzed close to him. He rolled in behind a deadfall that didn't give him complete protection, and lead chewed a large bite from it, showering him with moss and splinters.

'You sure made a helluva noise hackin' your way outta that ravine, Hardin!'

Hambone. As if to confirm, the young outlaw cut loose with his rooster call and Hardin pinpointed him. Coming up from the far side of the pool: must have ridden down the high trail after seeing or hearing him smashing a way through the brush, realized where he was headed, and found a way in.

Well, a way in also meant a way out.

Hambone triggered again and again, wasting lead, walking his shots along the slim deadfall, but forcing Hardin to keep his head down. When the echoes of the rifle-fire began to die away, Hardin spat bark and rotting grass and lifted his head slowly. He was startled to see Hambone riding in through the timber, standing in stirrups, sixgun now in hand. Hardin had to drop back smartly as the outlaw gave a rebel yell and lifted his running mount over the deadfall, shooting down at the same time. The drifter rolled away frantically, bringing his rifle up as he skidded on to his back. Ham was yanking the mount's head around as Hardin fired, levered, fired again.

Hambone was blasted out of the saddle and the horse ran off. The outlaw hit the ground with a thump, scrabbled around, bringing his sixgun to bear although he had both of Hardin's bullets in his lean body.

'Jer — said to — kill you . . . '

Hardin braced the scarred rifle butt into his hip and triggered twice. The shots lifted Hambone and sent him skidding to the edge of the pool, his gun falling from his grip, his eyes already dulling.

'Not today, Ham. Not this day.'

12

Pay-Off

Utah couldn't stand it any longer. He saw that Jericho was actually dozing in the saddle as they walked their mounts through the gold-and-blue afternoon of a perfect Colorado summer's day.

That bank bag slid back and forth across Jericho's saddle-flap with a slithering sound, the brass padlock catching the slanting sun's rays at the end of an arc, flashing, so that Utah saw it out of the corner of his eye every few seconds.

It was almost as if it was trying to get his attention. He swore softly and stepped his mount close alongside Jericho's. The outlaw leader came awake instantly, hand dropping to gun butt. He glared at Utah.

'The hell you doin'?'

'Jer, let's check that money. It's been worryin' me. We never took time to look and make sure it's all there.'

Jericho frowned. 'In a padlocked bank bag with a wire seal twisted through it? It'll take a bullet to bust that lock and I wasn't about to shoot it off and have the posse come down on my neck.'

'The posse likely wasn't nowheres near. C'mon, Jer. We're safe now. Anyway, you can cut into the bag's canvas, can't you?'

'They got wire woven through it but, yeah, OK. There's a waterhole just ahead.'

Jericho was right about the wire woven through the canvas. It blunted and resisted his Bowie knife but it only made him mad and he hacked and sawed and prised until he had a slit about six inches long in the canvas side of the bag, between the top and bottom bands of leather. Strands of wire poking out tore his hand as he reached in and brought out a neat bundle of green-backs, squared-off and wrapped around with the bank's paper sealing-strips. Blood oozed from the scratch and he swore, irritably tossed the bundle to Utah and worked his hand back inside the bag more carefully for another package.

'Looks like it's in hundred-dollar bills,' Jericho said, an edge of excitement and anticipation in his voice now.

Utah nodded, tearing away the bank bands, spreading out the bills. 'No, don't think they're hundreds. Looks more like — oh shit!'

Sucking the bleeding scratches, Jericho frowned across at the other man. 'The hell's the matter now — '

Anything else he had to say he swallowed as Utah silently fanned out the package and he saw that only the top bill was genuine money — a ten-dollar bill at that! The rest was just plain paper cut to size.

★ ★ ★

Hardin decided he might as well stay put in the clearing at the end of the ravine, even though he now had Ham's mount for his use. It would be full dark soon, earlier down here than on the mountain face, and he was one mass of aches and pains from battering his way through the tangled brush. He needed a good sleep, so he made sure both his guns were fully loaded, filled the loops in his cartridge belt from Ham's and ate the hardtack he found in the dead outlaw's saddle-bags. There was water in Ham's canteen and it sure tasted good, cleaner than the scummy stuff he had downed when he had first arrived.

He settled down with Ham's bedroll after covering the boy's body with rocks. But there was one thing that bothered him: Ham had lived for a little while and, afraid of dying, had talked incessantly, weakening his last reserves of strength rapidly.

Amongst all the stories from his life — a damned hard one because of his mental disability, it seemed, too — he had said more than once that Jericho still aimed to derail the train carrying 'Babe' DeLarue, the Carolina Songbird, as his way of thumbing his nose at the law.

Likely there was little that could be done, anyway, because Ham didn't know which rail track it was to use or the schedule. Thinking about it, Hardin figured Jericho wouldn't be likely to do the deed at night: he was the kind of crazy sonuver who would want to see every detail, so he would wait for daylight.

But it kept him awake for a time, despite his exhaustion, until, finally, he slept deeply as the sky coloured blood-red and clouds streamed out in intriguing patterns, the heavenly artwork all lost on the snoring drifter.

He awoke with a start as a hard boot crashed into his side. It was followed by another and he was kicked out of the bedroll by a third blow catching him on the left shoulder. He spilled awkwardly and tried to get his legs under him, but a knee rammed up against his forehead and catapulted him across the campsite.

His vision was flaring and blacking out alternately but he saw the man-shape coming after him with swinging fists. The old fighting instinct took over and Hardin crouched, fighting the pain in his body and throbbing head, ducking under a whistling blow. He came up inside the man's guard and whipped three lightning punches into the ribs.

The other grunted and stumbled as he stepped back hurriedly. Hardin went after him, crowding, keeping him off-balance, fists lashing out, a straight left, followed quickly by another, that snapped the man's head back, his hat flying, long hair swirling. A right hooked into the bruised ribs, another left landed in the same spot and, as the man sagged in the middle, Hardin's looping right fist slammed against his jaw. He heard teeth clash together and the man was going down, one hand reaching for the ground to keep from falling all the way.

'Utah!' the man croaked desperately. 'Where the — hell are — you . . . ?'

Hardin stopped at the sound of Jericho's agony-filled voice, spun as he heard a man crashing out of the brush behind him. Utah was mounted and rammed his horse at Hardin who shoulder-rolled and came up with his sixgun blazing.

Utah reeled in the saddle, his own gun stabbing flame angled down but wide of his target. He started to sag and he was vaguely silhouetted against the new dark, enough of a target for Hardin to drop flat, firing again.

Utah was smashed off the horse which ran on and, in its wild attempt to escape, crashed into the reeling Jericho. The outlaw was flung into the brush and the horse wheeled, blocking Hardin's intended shot. The drifter jumped back and tripped over the sprawled Utah. It was a scramble to get upright and by then Jericho was shooting.

Cole felt the air-whip of a slug passing his face and triggered, emptying his sixgun. Still groping against the ground in an effort to regain stability, he felt the rumpled edge of the blanket he had been sleeping on.

Holstering the sixgun he groped quickly, located his rifle with the battered butt and dived headlong as Jericho began shooting. The man had gotten a shotgun from somewhere — likely had laid it on the ground when he had first crept in and attacked Hardin with his boots. Utah's free and frightened horse whinnied, reared up, pawing the air, and then crashed away into the brush, whickering in pain as buckshot peppered its sweating hide.

Jericho used the animal's movements and sounds to cover his own rush to get closer to Hardin. The drifter rolled over and thrust to his knees, seeing Jericho's shape against the stars that were beginning to show through, bright enough to be seen clearly now.

The man was throwing down with

the shotgun when Hardin, rifle butt braced into his hip, worked the lever and trigger swiftly in three hammering shots. The outlaw was picked up and flung back, the shotgun thundering into the night, the muzzle blast starting a small fire in the leaves of a bush, but it died swiftly. Jericho was down, still thrashing. Hardin went forward, crouching, rifle cocked, saw the outlaw bringing up his Colt. He stomped viciously on the man's wrist, driving hand and gun brutally down into the soft leaf mould. Jericho groaned, wrenched once and then lay there panting. His breathing had a bubbling sound as Hardin knelt on one knee, tossed the sixgun out of reach.

'End of the trail for you, Jericho.'

The outlaw's eyes glared their hatred. The bloody lips worked and finally Hardin made out some of the words among the guttural curses coming out of the man's mouth.

'Double-crossin' — bastard! Fake — fake — money.'

Hardin was surprised. 'Didn't know that. But it stands to reason they'd try it.' Bitterly, he added, 'And I'd be the unlucky one within reach when you found out, not them.'

Jericho breathed raggedly, heavy, rasping half-grunts, half-sighs, staring up. 'You done — for — Ham.'

'Kid might've been touched but he was a killer.'

'Liked that — boy. Well — you got us — all now.' He managed to swivel his gaze to where Utah lay huddled and still. 'Wish you'd — joined us — man — like you . . .'

'Ham said you aimed to derail the train carrying Babe DeLarue.'

Jericho was silent except for the laboured breathing. 'Ham wanted to — see — a real — train crash.'

'You spoiled that kid, Jericho,' Hardin said sardonically. 'Anyway, it won't happen now.'

The sound was so strange, so mixed with explosive coughs that sprayed blood into the brush, and Jericho's body shook so much, that Hardin took some time to realize the man was trying to laugh!

He went cold, skin prickling with goosebumps. 'What's so damn funny?'

'Too — late — it's all fixed — train'll — crash anyway . . . '

By the time the full implication hit Hardin, Jericho was dead.

★   ★   ★

The herd had come together faster than Glory Carnavan expected. Having Hardin working a couple of days with Spud and the others had made a bigger difference than she would have thought. Then, when word came through that the meat agents were going to leave early for their packing houses in the north due to the heat of the summer, she decided to start the trail drive.

One agent, representing Hannis and Boyd Meat Packers in St Louis, told her that if she was willing to drive through Manitou Pass and down to the rail holding-pens at Whistler's Tanks watering stop, he would examine the herd and make her an offer on the spot. He had business to complete in Wildwood and could not spare the time to ride out to her spread. He had to be at the siding over at Lobo Drift in time to connect with the St Louis-bound train. It would be the last one for a week and he simply couldn't stand another seven days of this heat. Besides, his favourite actress was on board, the beautiful Carolina Songbird.

As she saw it, if she wanted cash in hand, this was the only way to do it. She had dealt with this particular agent before and was confident he would keep his word.

So she had recklessly promised her small crew a bonus to help get the herd underway. It took a lot of hard riding to bunch them for the drive, and Glory worked as hard as the four sweating cowboys. She could handle cattle as well as most cowpokes and she would ride along on the drive and see the men had good meals. They knew she was a good cook and that was a mighty important part of trail driving. More than one outfit had mutinied when the food was of poor quality. Even a short trail drive was a break from routine ranch chores and, if the agent gave Glory a decent price, the cowhands would get their promised bonus — a few dollars extra were always welcome.

She started the drive before daylight. The cattle were already resting in the creek pasture so it was only a matter of dropping the fence wire and starting them moving. There were protests and loud bellowing but no real hassles as the cows were wakened and set walking right away.

There was plenty of noise and lots of dust but there would be heaps more of each before the short run to Whistler's Tanks was over. She was tense and anxious, hoping the train wouldn't arrive before her. It was an unscheduled run, and she was grateful: without it she would miss out altogether on the sale of her herd.

It was a hot, gruelling drive to the pass, the cattle wanting to veer over towards the river all the time. The five riders had their work cut out and Glory began to wonder if they would make the Tanks in time after all. Dust clouds turned a bright morning into half-twilight.

On the south side of the pass she saw a lone rider coming out of the heat haze towards the herd and her stomach clenched. Riding point, she looked around quickly: Spud was having some trouble with the drag, a slight milling of cranky steers; Stoke and Crabb were busy, too, on the left wing — there was a downer and the animal resisted all efforts to get it on its feet again. Pedro was off chasing a brace of break-aways.

Swinging her gaze to the rider, she squinted, shaded her eyes. That looked like a palomino . . .

Her heart began to beat faster: *Yes!* It was Cole Hardin! She felt herself flush with a surge of excitement at sight of the drifter. He was riding kind of funny, though . . . Then she saw that he was sitting slightly to the left, favouring that side.

She spurred her grey forward, waving. He waved back and they met by a rock that radiated heat from six feet away.

'Saw your dust cloud but figured it was a wind storm blowing up at first,' Hardin said, his face showing signs of bruising and swelling beneath the film of grime, a legacy from hard riding. 'I'm sure glad to see you, Glory.'

She knew her flush deepened but she smiled warmly. 'I'm glad you got back safely. Any trouble delivering that money to Jericho?'

Before she had finished the question she saw by his face that he had a story to tell. And he told it swiftly, repeating some of it again. He looked at the girl grimly.

'We've got to stop that train, Glory. Jericho's already undermined the track somewhere. For all I know it could've already hit it and crashed.'

'Oh, Lord, I hope not!' And she told him briefly why they were driving the herd through the pass. 'I'd like to find the train waiting safely at Whistler's Tanks.' She glanced up at the sky. 'We'll be hard-put to get there on time.'

'Well, if it gets that far safely there's no problem for anyone, but if Jericho and his crew sabotaged the track on the approach side of the Tanks . . . '

'You'd better ride on ahead, Cole,' she told him. 'You can warn them and hold the train for us if it's there.'

Hardin nodded. 'Point me in the right direction. I had one helluva job getting out of that ravine and Jericho rode the palomino damned hard. Is it far?'

She pointed to a knoll rising out of the sea of shimmering heat. 'A few miles beyond the knoll. It's mostly rolling prairie. They'll see you coming from a long way off.'

'Which may or may not be a good thing.' Hardin told her. 'They'll be edgy after that freight-train crash and will likely have armed guards travelling on board. They'll be mighty leery of anyone trying to flag the train down.'

'If only we knew where Jericho had weakened the track!'

'And if horses could fly we'd be at the train in a few minutes. We're wasting time, Glory. See you at the Tanks.'

He lifted a hand, turned the palomino sharply and spurred away towards the knoll.

Glory Carnavan rode back quickly towards the herd which had decided to stop and enjoy some of the shade cast by the high walls of the pass. Worriedly, she wondered how long it would take to get them moving again. The money they represented meant a great deal to her future.

★　★　★

Hardin saw the smoke trail laying a black streak across the horizon when he topped the knoll and knew he stood a good chance of reaching the Tanks ahead of the train. Then he sobered.

It was a long way off yet, and there were miles of glittering silver rail track between the tanks and the approaching loco. It would need only a few feet of that throbbing iron to have been loosened from its ties, or the joining plates to have been removed, and the train would be doomed.

The palomino was sweating, obviously weary, as he was. But it was a fine horse, co-operative and obliging, even after the several different riders it had endured these past couple of weeks. Hardin touched the spurs to the satiny golden flanks and the animal knew at once what was wanted of it. He actually felt the slight hesitation before the bulging of the tensing muscles and their smooth flowing as the animal stretched out, long legs eating at the distance.

The hot wind did nothing to make their passage easier and the motion in the saddle sent stabs of pain through

Hardin's battered body. Water streamed from his already reddened eyes. He stood in the stirrups as the palomino flew down the slope of the knoll and hit the prairie, rolling away towards the distant streak of the railroad tracks. He thought he heard a faint scream which was probably the engineer blowing the loco's whistle, maybe at some animal on the track, forcing it to give right of way. The smoke seemed to be thicker so he figured this meant the train was going faster and he swallowed a curse.

Faster was what he didn't want right now! It would only close the gap between the train and the sabotaged rails more quickly. How the hell was he going to tell where Jericho and his pards had prised up the track or sheared away the bolt-heads on the joining plates?

There would be no obvious sign from way back here: a man would have to ride — no, walk — along the rails if he wanted to detect the break. Certainly the engineer would never spot anything wrong until too late.

He would have to try to get on board and convince the driver to stop the train while the rails were examined. That was easier said than done.

He rode straight in for the rails where they crossed his path. Get close, ride back towards the train, signal like hell to make the engineer stop. If the man wouldn't — or couldn't — maybe he could sit the palomino between the rails and hope the man out of plain humanity would slam on the brakes.

But what if the engineer had been ordered not to stop for any reason? It had happened on the stages when hold-ups were frequent in the south-west. Tight orders came down from Head Office: the stage was not to stop for anything or pick up anyone, only at the designated waystations. No matter what the reason — apparent accident, or lost traveller, injured man or woman: *nothing*. The risk of a hold-up was too great.

If the train driver had been similarly

instructed, he was going to have hell's own job keeping that train from crashing.

He had closed in faster than he had thought while worrying about what he was going to do. There was the train streaking and clanking towards him down a straight section of track, rocking and swaying with the speed, whistle shrieking. The palomino had slowed a lot and was beginning to stagger a little, ears flicking with each blast of the whistle.

'Just one more effort, boy. Just a little more!'

He stood in the stirrups, waved his hat. The train didn't slow even a fraction. He wasn't even certain they had seen him. Then, not thinking, he unsheathed the rifle, figuring a few shots would get their attention.

It did: but not from the driver. Suddenly guns appeared at the windows of the passenger cars and there was a rattle of gunfire and puffs of dust spitting around the stamping feet of the palomino, some beyond him on a slight rise. Hell! What a fool he was! Drawing his gun like that!

They thought he was trying to hold-up the damn train! He started to run the palomino towards the loco, alongside the track, but the guns blasted again and the lead this time was way too close.

Then he saw it! The blue metal rail bed had been raised and built up here across a hollow so as to keep the rails as level as possible. He saw where two rails had been moved a few inches out of line. They must have used a cold chisel to cut off the burred-over tops of the heavy rivets holding the plates that joined the rails together. Then they prised the plates off, levered the rails slightly apart, enough for a speeding train to hit them with a spinning wheel which would hurl the rail aside like a flying spear.

Then there would be nowhere for the train to go but over the edge of the raised railbed and a hundred tons of driving, steaming steel would plough into the earth, dragging the cars behind it until they all cannonballed, smashing into each other, end-to-end, like a dreadful concertina, splintering, shattering, bouncing across the prairie, pulping every living thing inside.

The thoughts literally flashed through his head. He waved frantically, sitting the palomino between the tracks, but the animal was not going to co-operate for that. Already afraid and tired beyond what could normally be expected of it, the horse defied his signals and plunged away from the track. It slid and almost fell down the sloping blue metal and by the time he had regained control, he knew he was too late. He couldn't stop the train now: it was roaring and charging along the track like a runaway. And the men were still shooting at him.

He snapped his head around as he heard the sudden bawling of cattle. Hardin blinked and fought the reins as the herd came thundering towards him in stampede — a driven stampede, Glory and her cowboys hazing the wild-eyed cows across the tracks.

He stared, jaw dropping a little. If the train ploughed into that living river of beef there would be one hell of a blood bath — literally!

'God almighty!' he breathed, wrenching the palomino away from the trembling rails.

The train was no more than a hundred and fifty yards away now, not slowing down any, and even from here he saw the whiteness of Glory's face as she realized her gamble wasn't going to pay off. She was going to lose half her herd in a terrible, bloody slaughter and probably the train would derail anyway with all that solid beef jamming under the wheels. The whistle screamed and the herd seemed to shudder like one huge entity, horns tossing, nostrils spurting streams of mucus, eyes rolling. The cows tried to veer away from the train but —

Showers of sparks spurted from

under the loco's wheels now. The engineer was hanging out of his window, almost past the point of balance, waving frantically, his face grey as he waited for the crash and the terrible mangling it would mean.

The stream of cattle, in blind panic, kept coming, following the leaders over the rails: a frantic living river. The locomotive skidded, thrust forward by the massive tonnage of the cars and open freight wagons behind, bore down on them. The noise was tremendous: the clanking of the train's couplings and the screeching ring of hot metal wheels sliding over the rails, the bawling of the cattle, the drowned-out shouting of the men, even a few gunshots fired by some panicked guard on board, trying to frighten off the crazed steers.

Hardin simply sat the trembling palomino, stroking its sweat-sleek neck now, awaiting the inevitable as the roaring tons of smoking iron reached out to mangle hide and horn and flesh . . . but it never happened.

The train rocked to a precarious stop not five yards from the rushing stream of cattle leaping the rails in front of the well-named cow-catcher . . . a few slipped or stumbled on the rails and died but the vast majority stayed clear. Hardin saw Glory slump in her saddle and wondered if she had fainted. He had thought for a time there he might join her . . .

* * *

'Anyone who would take such a risk, put their life and livelihood on the line so as to give other people a chance of living, well, he — or she! — deserves to be rewarded.'

Matheson, the meat agent, was speaking amongst the crowd that now stood beside the panting train, chattering, all eyes on Glory and her cowboys, a few on Hardin. They were the centre of attention even above the crinoline beauty of Babe DeLarue, who waited, shaded by a lace-edged umbrella, some of her retinue gathering around her.

'Miss Carnavan,' the agent went on, 'I am prepared to pay you top dollar for your herd. You have lost at least a dozen, maybe more, in your gallant attempt to save our lives, but I will even pay for the dead animals.' He lifted his eyes to the distant knoll where a line of curious Indians sat their ponies with lances raised and shields in hands. 'Perhaps we can leave the meat for them . . . ?'

Glory smiled and came and stood beside Hardin as the agent, carried away now in the utter relief at deliverance from what had seemed like certain death, began addressing the crowd, telling them they had seen a practical demonstration of what fortitude and courage good, red beef could instil in a person who had plenty in their diet.

Hardin and the girl moved away as Spud and the other cowhands did what they could to keep the herd more or less together.

'I think we worked well together, Cole.'

He smiled. 'Reckon so.'

'Are your feet still itching?'

He looked down into her expectant face and after a moment, smiled. 'Might stick around a spell.'

'Would you stay and work for me? Until you felt you had to move on, of course . . . '

He didn't reply, just broadened his smile. She moved closer to him and after a brief pause, he felt her hand warm and firm in his.

★ ★ ★

Borden had hurriedly closed the bank and gone home as soon as he was given the news that his house on the hill outside of town was ablaze, but his family was safe.

Macauley was in his hotel room, packing, when The Major came in with a telegraph message form in his hand. There was ash caught on the brim of his hat and a little more on his shirt-front. He waved the message and opened the envelope. Macauley silently closed one leather valise. He had already had a wire from the railroad company's head office, demanding his immediate return, 'pending an enquiry into his recent activities and some missing confidential company papers, proposed new timetables and map . . . '

'My God! They — they're not happy with our performance, Major! The railroad suspect I have been divulging 'extremely confidential' matters to out-side 'interests', meaning The Group, of course.'

The Major looked up from his message. 'Guess so. I paid the Borden house a visit at the request of The Group.' He paused to sniff the air and its tang of smoke, waved his telegraph form again. Macauley's lips tightened. 'I'm ordered back to Chicago, too. But I don't quite understand the end of the message . . . '

Macauley frowned at the strange

touch of bantering in The Major's voice. The killer held out the message form, a finger on his free hand indicating the words.

'*Close down?*' Macauley read. 'Why, that's self-evident. It means close down the operation entirely and tie up any loose ends that — ' His face was very grey and lined now as he choked on the words, snapping his eyes to The Major's face. 'Oh my God!'

He stared down the muzzle of The Major's sixgun only inches from his eyes, the cold smile on the man's face slightly out of focus.

'Tell me what it feels like to be a 'loose end', Mr Macauley . . . '

THE END

SILVER GALORE

John Dyson

The mysterious southern belle, Careen Langridge, has come West to escape death threats from fanatical Confederates. Is she still being pursued? Should she marry Captain Robbie Randall? The Mexican Artiside Luna has his own plans ... With gambler and fast-gun Luke Short he murders Randall's men and targets Careen. Can the amiable cowboy Tex Anderson and his pal, Pancho, impose rough justice as with guns blazing they go to Careen's aid?

CARSON'S REVENGE

Jim Wilson

When the Mexican bandit General Rodriguez hangs Carson's grandfather, the youngster vows revenge, and with that aim joins the Texas Rangers. Then as Carson escorts Mexican Henrietta Xavier to her home, Rodriguez kidnaps her. The ranger plucks the heiress from the general's clutches, and the youngsters make a desperate run for the border and safety. Will Carson's strength and courage be enough to save them as he tries to get the better of the brutal general and his bandits?

INCIDENT AT COYOTE WELLS

Logan Winters

John Magadan escapes the hangman's noose, but his ride through the Sonora Desert bristles with violence and danger: he's pursued by Sheriff Tom Driscoll's posse; the Corson gang want the treasure which they feel they have been cheated out of; the Yaqui Indians want his horse and his blood. Beth Tolliver knows that Magadan holds the key to free her brother from Yuma prison — and something else . . . and she's decided that Magadan will stay to the bitter, bloody end.